Collages

COLLAGES

a novel by

Anais Nin

THE **SWALLOW PRESS** INC.
CHICAGO

Published by
The Swallow Press, Inc.
1139 S. Wabash Avenue
Chicago, Illinois 60605

ISBN 0-8040-0045-X
LIBRARY OF CONGRESS CATALOG CARD NUMBER 64-25338

To R. P.

For the real gardener
who created a world in which
a humorous book could bloom

VIENNA WAS THE CITY OF STATUES. THEY WERE AS NUMEROUS AS the people who walked the streets. They stood on the top of the highest towers, lay down on stone tombs, sat on horseback, kneeled, prayed, fought animals and wars, danced, drank wine and read books made of stone. They adorned cornices like the figureheads of old ships. They stood in the heart of fountains glistening with water as if they had just been born. They sat under the trees in the parks summer and winter. Some wore costumes of other periods, and some no clothes at all. Men, women, children, kings, dwarfs, gargoyles, unicorns, lions, clowns, heroes, wise men, prophets, angels, saints and soldiers preserved for Vienna an illusion of eternity.

As a child Renate could see them from her bedroom window. At night, when the white muslin curtains fluttered out like ballooning wedding dresses, she heard them whispering like figures which had been petrified by a spell during the day and came alive only at night. Their silence by day taught her to read their frozen lips as one reads the messages of deaf mutes. On rainy days their granite eye sockets shed tears mixed with soot.

Renate would never allow anyone to tell her the history of the statues, or to identify them. This would have situated them in the past. She was convinced that people did not die, they became statues. They were people under a spell and if she were watchful enough they would tell her who they were and how they lived *now*.

Renate's eyes were sea green and tumultuous like a reduction of the sea itself. When they seemed about to overflow with emotion, her laughter would flutter like windchimes and form a crystal bowl to contain the turquoise waters as if in an aquarium, and then her eyes became scenes of Venice, canals of reflections, and gold specks swam in them like gondolas. Her long black hair was swept away from her face into a knot at the top of her head, then fell over her shoulders.

7

Renate's father built telescopes and microscopes, so that for a long time Renate did not know the exact size of anything. She had only seen them diminutive or magnified.

Renate's father treated her like a confidante, a friend. He took her with him on trips, to the inauguration of telescopes, or to ski. He discussed her mother with her as if Renate were a woman, and explained that it was her mother's constant depression which drove him away from home.

He relished Renate's laughter, and there were times when Renate wondered whether she was not laughing for two people, laughing for herself but also for her mother who never laughed. She laughed even when she felt like weeping.

When she was sixteen she decided she wanted to become an actress. She informed her father of this while he was playing chess, hoping that his concentration on the game would neutralize his reaction. But he dropped his king and turned pale.

Then he said very coldly and quietly: "But I have watched you in your school plays and I do not think you are a good actress. You only acted an exaggerated version of yourself. And besides, you're a child, not a woman yet. You looked as if you had dressed up in your mother's clothes for a masquerade."

"But, Father, it was you who once said that what you liked about actresses was that they were exaggerated women! And now you use this very phrase against me, to pass judgment on me."

Renate spoke vehemently, and as she spoke her sense of injustice grew magnified. It took the form of a long accusation.

"You have always loved actresses. You spend all your time with them. I saw you one night working on a toy based on an interplay of mirrors. I thought it was for me. I was the one who liked to look through kaleidoscopes. But you gave it to an actress. Once you would not take me to the theater, you said I was too young, yet you took a girl from my school, and she showed me all the flowers and candy you sent her. You just want to keep me a child forever, so I will stay in the house and cheer you up."

She did not talk like a child angry that her father did not believe in her talent, but like a betrayed wife or mistress.

8

She stormed and grew angrier until she noticed that her father had grown paler, and was clutching at his heart. Frightened, she stopped herself short, ran for the medicine she had seen him take, gave him the drops, and then kneeled beside him and said softly: "Father, Father, don't be upset. *I was only pretending.* I was putting on an act to prove to you that I could be a good actress. You see, you believed me, and it was all pretence."

These words softly spoken, revived her father. He smiled feebly and said: "You're a much better actress than I thought you were. You really frightened me."

Out of guilt she buried the actress. It was only much later she discovered that her father had long been ill, that she had not been told, and that it was not this scene which had brought on the first symptoms of a weak heart.

In every relationship, sooner or later, there is a court scene. Accusations, counter-accusations, a trial, a verdict.

In this scene with her father, Renate condemned the actress to death thinking that her guilt came from opposing his will. It was only later that she became aware that this had not been a trial between father and daughter.

She had, for a few moments, taken the place of her mother and voiced accusations her mother had never uttered. Her mother had been content to brood, or to weep. But Renate had spoken unconsciously a brief for an unloved wife.

It had not been the rebellion of a daughter against a father's orders she felt guilty of, but her assuming what should have been her mother's role and place in her father's heart.

And her father too, she knew now, had not been hurt by a daughter's rebellion, but by the unmasking of a secret: he had not looked upon Renate as a daughter but as a woman, and his insistence on maintaining her a child was to disguise the companionship he enjoyed.

After this scene, Renate's father searched for a tutor because Renate had at the same time refused to continue to go to school.

He had a brother who had refused to go to school and had locked himself up in his room with many books. He only came out of it to eat and to renew his supply of books. At the end of seven years he came out and passed his examinations brilliantly and became a professor.

He indulged in one gentle form of madness which did not affect his scholarly and philosophical knowledge. He insisted that he had no marrow in his bones.

Renate's father thought that his brother would be a good tutor for Renate. He could teach her music, painting, and languages. It would help to keep her at home, away from the influence of other girls. But he explained the professor's obsession to her, and stressed clearly that she must never refer to bones or marrow as it ignited his irrational obsession.

Renate was naturally strongly tempted to discuss this very mystifying theme, and the marrow madness of her uncle interested her far more than anything else he might teach her.

She spent many days trying to find a tactful way to introduce this theme in their talks together. She did some preparatory research in the library. She discovered that birds have no marrow in their bones. She bought her uncle a canary with a coloratura voice and said: "Did you know that birds do not have marrow in their bones?"

"Yes," said her uncle, "but neither have I."

"How marvelous," said Renate, "that means that you can fly!"

Her uncle was impressed but would not put himself through the test. For fear she might urge him to explore this new concept, he never referred to his handicap again. But before adopting complete silence on this subject he offered her a rational explanation of its cause.

"My mother told me that she became pregnant while still nursing me. Slowly I realized that this other child, my brother, had absorbed all the nourishment away from me, thus leaving me without marrow in my bones."

When Bruce first came to Vienna Renate noticed him because of his resemblance to one of the statues which smiled at her through her bedroom window. It was the statue with wings on its heels, the one she was convinced travelled during the night. She observed him every morning while eating her breakfast. She was certain she could detect signs of long journeys. His hair seemed more ruffled, there was mud on his winged feet.

She recognized in Bruce the long neck, the runner's legs, the lock of hair over the forehead.

But Bruce denied this relationship to Mercury. He thought of himself as Pan. He showed Renate how long the downy hair was at the tip of his ears.

Familiarity with the agile, restless statue put her at ease with Bruce. What added to the resemblance was that Bruce talked little. Or he talked with motions of his body and the gestures were more eloquent than the words. He entered into conversation with a forward thrust of his shoulders, as if he were going either to fly or swim into its current, and when he could not find the words he would shake his body as if he were executing a jazz dance which would shake them out like dice. His thoughts were still enclosed within his body and could only be transmitted through it. The words he was about to say first shook his body and one could follow their course in the vibrations running through it, in the shuffling rhythm of his feet. Gusts of words agitated every muscle, but finally converged into one, at the most two words: "Man, see, man, see here, man, oh man."

At other times they rushed out in rhythmic patterns like variations in jazz so swift one could barely catch them. He was looking for words equivalent to jazz rhythms. He was impatient with sequences, chronology, and construction. An interruption seemed to him more eloquent than a complete paragraph.

But Renate, having been trained for years to read the unmoving lips of statues, heard the words which came from the perfect

11

modelling of Bruce's lips. The message she heard was: "What does one do when one is fourteen times removed from one's true self, not two, or three, but fourteen times away from the center?"

She would start with making a portrait of him. He would see himself as she saw him. That would be a beginning.

They worked together for many afternoons. What Bruce observed was compassion in her voice, what he saw under her heavy sensual eyelids was a diminutive image of himself swimming in the film of emotion which humidified her eyes.

"Come with me to Mexico," said Bruce. "I want to wander about a little until I find out who I am, what I am."

And so they started on a trip together. Bruce wanted to put space and time between the different cycles of his life.

It was during the long drives through hot deserts, the meals at small saffron-perfumed restaurants on the road, the walks through the prismatic markets to the tune of soft Mexican chants that he said, as Renate's father had said: "I love to hear you laughing, Renate."

If the heavy rains caught them in their finest clothes, on the way to a bullfight, Renate laughed as if the gods, Mexican or others, were playing pranks. If there were no more hotel rooms, and if by listening to the advice of the barman they ended in a whorehouse, Renate laughed. If they arrived late at night, and there was a sandstorm blowing, and no restaurants open, Renate laughed.

"I want to bring all this back with us," she said once.

"But what is this?" asked Bruce.

"I am not sure. I only know I want to bring it back with us and live according to it."

"I know what it is," said Bruce, spilling the contents of their valises over the beds, and searching for the alarm clock. Then he repacked negligently, and as they drove away, a few hours later, on a deserted road, he stopped, wound up the alarm clock, and left it standing on the middle of the road. As they drove away, it suddenly became unleashed like an angry child, the alarm bell rang like a tantrum, and it shook with fury and protest at neglect.

Sometimes they stopped late at night in a motel which looked like a hacienda. The gigantic old ovens, shaped like cones, had been turned into bedrooms. The *brasero* in the center of the tent-shaped room threw its smoke to the converging opening at the top. The cold stone was covered with red and black *serapes*. Renate would brush her long hair. Bruce would go out without a word. His exit was like a vanishing act, because he made no announcement, and was followed by silence. And this silence was not like an intermission. It was like a premonition of death. The image of his pale face vanishing gave her the feeling of someone seeking to be warmed by moonlight. The Mexican sun could not tan him. He had already been permanently tinted by the Norwegian midnight sun of his parents' native country.

From occasional vague descriptions, Renate had understood that his parents had brought him up in this impenetrable silence. They had a language they talked between themselves and had only a broken form of English to use with the child. They had left him in America at the age of eleven, without any words of explanation, returned to Norway, and let him be brought up by a distant relative.

"Distant he was," said Bruce once, laughing. "My first job was given to me by a neighbor who owned the candy machines in which kids put a penny and get candy and sometimes if they are lucky, a prize. The prizes were rings, small whistles, tin soldiers, a new penny, a tie pin. My job was to insert a little glue so the prizes would never come down the slot."

They laughed.

"When I met you in Vienna, I was on my way to see my parents. Then I thought: what's the use? I don't even remember their faces."

Before he had left the room, they had been drinking Mexican beer. He said looking at his glass and turning it in his hand: "When you are drunk an ordinary glass shines like a diamond."

Renate added: "When you are drunk an iron bed seems like the feather bed of sensual Sultans."

He rebelled against all ties, even the loving web of words,

13

promises, compliments. He left without announcing his return, not even using the words most people uttered every day: "I'll be seeing you!"

Renate would fall asleep in her orange shawl, forgetting to undress. At first she slept, and then awakened and waited. But waiting in a Mexican hotel in the middle of the desert with only the baying of dogs, the flutter of palm trees by candlelight, seemed ominous. And so one night she went in search of him.

The countryside was dark, filled with fireflies and the hum of cicadas. There was only one small café lit with orange oil lamps. Peasants in dirty white suits sat drinking. A guitarist was playing and singing slowly, as if sleep had half-hypnotized him. Bruce was not there.

Returning along the dark road she saw a shadow by a tree. A car passed by. Its headlight illumined the side of the road and two figures standing by a tree. A young Mexican boy stood leaning against the vast tree trunk, and Bruce was kneeling before him. The Mexican boy rested his dark hand on Bruce's blond hair and his face was raised towards the moon, his mouth open.

Weeping Renate ran back to the room, packed and drove away.

She drove to Puerta Maria by the sea where they were exhibiting her paintings. And the image of the night tree with its flowers of poison was replaced by her first sight of a coral tree in the glittering sunlight.

It eclipsed all the other trees with the intensity of its orange flowers growing in tight wide bouquets at the end of bare branches, so that there were no leaves or shadows of leaves to attenuate the explosion of colors. They had petals which seemed made of ,orange fur tipped with blood-red tendrils. It was the flower from the coral tree which should have been named the passion flower.

As soon as she saw it she wanted a dress of that color and that intensity. That was not difficult to find in a Mexican sea town. All their dresses took their colors from flowers. She bought the coral tree dress. The orange cotton had almost invisible blood-red

14

threads running through it as if the Mexicans had concocted their dyes from the coral tree flower itself.

The coral tree would kill the memory of a black gnarled tree and of two figures sheltered under its grotesque branches.

The coral tree would carry her into a world of festivities. An orange world.

In Haiti the trees were said to walk at night. Many Haitians swore they had actually seen them move, or had found them in different places in the morning. So at first she felt as if the coral tree had moved from its birthplace and was walking through the spicy streets or the dazzling festive beach. Her own starched, flouncing skirt made her think of the coral tree flower that never wilted on the tree, but at death fell with a sudden stab to earth.

The coral tree dress did not fray or fade in the tropical humidity. But Renate did not, as she had expected, become suffused with its colors. She had hoped to be penetrated by the orange flames and that it would dye her mood to match the joyous life of the sea town. She had thought that steeped in its fire she would be able to laugh with the orange gaiety of the natives. She had expected to absorb its liveliness intravenously. But to the self that had sought to disguise her regrets the coral tree dress remained a costume.

Every day the dress became more brilliant, drenched in sunlight and matching its dazzling hypnosis. But Renate's inner landscape was not illumined by it. Inside her grew a gigantic, tortured black tree and two young men who had made a bed of it.

People stopped her as she passed, women to envy, children to touch, men to receive the magnetic rays. On the beach, people turned towards her as if the coral tree itself had come walking down the hill.

But inside the dress lay a black tree, the night. How people were taken in by symbolism! She felt like a fraud, drawing everyone into her circle of orange fire.

She attracted the attention of a man from Los Angeles who wore white sailor pants, a white T-shirt, and who was suntanned and smiling at her.

Is he truly happy, she wondered, or is he wearing a disguise too?

At the beach he had merely smiled. But here in the market, the one behind the bullring, he was lost, and he appealed to her. He did not know where he was. His arms were full of straw hats, straw donkeys, pottery, baskets and sandals.

He had strayed among the parrots, the sliced and odorous melons, the women's petticoats and ribbons. The petticoats swollen by the breeze caressed his hair and damp cheeks. The palm-leafed roofs were too low for him and the tips of the leaves tickled his ears.

"I must get back soon," he said. "I left my car alone for two hours now."

"They're not strict with tourists," she answered. "Don't worry."

"Oh, it's not in the street. I wouldn't leave it in the street. I tried every hotel in town, until I found one where I could park my car near my bedroom. Do you want to come and see it?"

He said this in the tone of a man offering a glimpse of an original Picasso.

They walked slowly in the sun. "It's such a beautiful car," he said, "the best they ever made. I raced it in Los Angeles. It's as sensitive as a human being. You don't know what an ordeal it was, the trip from Mexico City. They are repairing the road—it was full of detours."

"What happened to you?"

"Nothing happened to me, but my poor car! I could feel every bump on the road, every hole, the dust, the stones. It hurt me to see it struggle along that road, scraped by pebbles, stained with tar, covered with red dust, my beautiful car that I took such care of. It was as if my own body were walking on that road. I had to drive through a river. A little boy sat astride the hood, and guided me with a propeller-like gesture of his hand, indicating the best path through the water. But I never knew when we were going to get stuck there, my poor low-slung car in muddied waters, where the natives wash all their laundry, and bathe the

16

cattle. I could feel the sand and grit in the motor. I could see the flies, mosquitoes, and other insects cluttering the air vent. I never want to put my car through such an experience again."

They had reached a low, wide rambling hotel surrounded by a vast jungle garden. There under a palm tree, among sun flowers and ferns, stood the car, sleek and shining, seemingly undamaged.

"Oh, it's in the sun," cried the man from Los Angeles and rushed to move it into shadows. "It's a good thing I came back. Do you want to sit in it? I'll order drinks meanwhile."

He held the door open.

Renate said: "I would love to drive to the beach on the other side of the mountain. It's beautiful at this time of the day."

"I've heard of it, but it wouldn't be good for the car. They're building on that road. I hear them set off dynamite. I wouldn't trust Mexicans with dynamite."

"Have you been to the bullfight?"

"I can't take my car there, the boys steal tires and side mirrors, I hear."

"Have you been to the Black Pearl night club?"

"That's one place we can go to, they have a parking lot with an attendant. Yes, I'll take you there."

Later when they were having a drink, the sun descended like a meteorite of antique gold and sank into the sea.

"Ha," breathed the man, smiling. "I'm glad it's cooler now. The sun is not good for my car."

Then he explained that for the return home he had made arrangements to get his car back without suffering anymore. "I booked passage on a freighter. It will take three weeks. But it will be easier on my car."

"Be sure and buy a big bottle of mineral water," said Renate.

"To wash the car?" asked the man from Los Angeles, frowning.

"No, for yourself. You might get dysentery."

She offered to speak to the captain of the freighter because she talked Spanish.

They drove to the docks together. The captain stood half-

17

naked directing the loading of bananas and pineapples. He wore a handkerchief tied to his forehead to keep the perspiration from falling over his face. The orange dress attracted his eyes and he smiled.

Renate asked him if he would consent to share his cabin with the American, and take good care of him.

"Anything to please the señorita," he said.

"How will you fare on fish and black beans?" she asked the car worshipper.

"Let's buy some canned food, and a sponge to wash the salt off my car. It will be on the open deck."

The day of his departure the beach town displayed its most festive colors; the parrots whistled, the magnolia odors covered the smell of fish, and the flowers were as profuse as at a New Orleans Carnival.

Renate arrived in time to see the car being measured and found too big for the net in which they usually picked up the cargo. So they placed two narrow planks from the pier to the deck, and the man was asked to drive the car onto the freighter. One inch out of the way and both car and man would fall into the bay. But the owner of the car was a skilful driver, and an amorous one, so he finally maneuvered it on deck. Once there, it was found to be so near the edge that the sailors had to rope it tightly like a rebellious bronco. Lashed to the ship by many ropes it could no longer roll over the edge.

Then the man from Los Angeles moved into the only cabin with his big bottle of mineral water and a bag of canned soups.

As the freighter slowly tugged away he cried: "I'll let you know in what state my car gets there! Thanks for your help."

A month later she received a letter:

Dear Kind Friend: I will always remember you so gay and carefree in your orange dress. And how wise you were! If only I had listened to your warnings! I used the mineral water to wash the salty mist off my car, and so the first thing that happened was that I got the 'tourista' with a high fever. The captain kept his word to you and shared his cabin with me, but also with a barrel of fish, cans of gasoline, and hay for the animals. Then the sea got pretty rough and the car began to roll back and forth, and at each roll I thought it would plunge into the sea. I decided to sleep inside it, and if anything were to happen we would both go together. At the first town we stopped at, we took in a herd of cattle. They were crowded on deck, and they pushed against my car, dribbled on it, and even tried to gore it. At night they quarrelled and I don't need to describe the stench. The heat was as heavy as a blanket. At the second stop we took in a Madame and about twenty call girls who were being moved to another house. The captain gallantly offered his cabin. Tequila was free on board and so you can imagine how rowdy the nights were. After three weeks I arrived in Los Angeles a wreck, but my car is in fine shape. I had it lubricated and I wish you could hear it purr along the roads. Los Angeles has such wonderful roads.

Weeks later, when she was installed in her house, Bruce arrived, as if they had agreed to take a detour and resume their relationship. He laid his dusty and tired head on her shoulder and sought in the darkest part of her hair, at the base of her neck, the place where the nerves most clearly carried messages of future pleasures. His eyes were clear and innocent, free of memories. He smiled innocently, and settled in the house like a privileged guest, detached from the care of it. He took the cover off his typewriter, and then he gave her a few pages to read.

"That's the beginning of my novel," he said.

And Renate read:

> The hotel in Acapulco was a series of cottages. It seems the 'patron' was quite a puritan and wanted no scandal, no extra visitors at night. It seemed that he patrolled the cottages at night himself. He wanted the place to remain a 'family' hotel.

Renate interrupted with: "But that's the hotel where I stayed."
"Read on."

> A woman arrived in an orange dress. It was not only the orange dress which aroused attention. She radiated joy and her laughter was warm and spontaneous. The patron knew she was alone and he often hovered around her cottage to catch the foreigner at some unholy hospitality. One night there was a man's laughter mingled with hers, but the 'patron' did not hear it. A neighbor heard it. He stayed awake to listen, saying to himself he must warn the girl in the orange dress if the 'patron' came near. She was fortunate. The man remembered being all stirred up by the laughter, by the intimate quality of it. And the next morning he examined the girl in the orange dress with more attention, as if he had failed to notice in her face or in her behavior what would create such laughter at night. She was having breakfast, with her eyelids lowered. And then a chambermaid came in, breathless, and talked to the

'patron', and the 'patron' came and talked to the girl in the orange dress, and the girl got up blushing and rushed away. It seems that she had left the visitor early in the morning, that he was to have dressed quietly, unobtrusively, and be gone by the time she came back. But as she left, she unconsciously locked the screen door and imprisoned him, so that he had to call the maid, and the maid, thinking she had trapped a bootlegged occupant had reported him while he rattled the door in anger and thus let everyone know . . .

Renate began to laugh. She laughed until Bruce began to laugh with her, though he was not as certain of the meaning of the incident as she was.

She saw that he was laughing from contagion, with trust in her comic spirit, and this made her laugh all the more as a touching form of love.

"I must have been thinking of you, Bruce. You, and how quietly you slipped away at night. It must have been you I wanted to lock up!"

"Did you love him?"

Renate laughed. "He looked like Pinocchio at the piano, but sang like Caruso, only more lightly. He was just back from visiting his mother, so beautiful he said, with a luminous skin and eyes just like mine. He had her all to himself, he told me, his brothers and sisters being married, and he loved her, he realized he loved her (and me because I resembled her) so much in the way Freud said!"

A few days later she brought Bruce a peace dove she had found pinned to the wall of a Swedish shop. It was carved out of paper-thin wood with transparent wings as light as a breath.

Renate said: "Let's hang it up by a thread so it will spin."

Bruce climbed on a ladder and began to hang it up. He asked Renate for thread which she brought him. It broke. The peace dove fell to the ground. Bruce said: "Now I know why my buttons never stay on. You sew them with such a weak thread."

Renate brought stronger thread. She went to light a fire in

the fireplace. She prepared dinner. She prepared food for the dogs, Tequila and Sake.

"Why didn't you buy a whole flock of doves? I would have liked a whole flock of doves flying around the room."

"A whole flock of doves wouldn't bring peace to our relationship."

"You know the consequences of opening Pandora's box," he said.

"You never give me any warning of your departures. You call all amenities balls and chains. You take the only car we have so that I cannot even escape."

"To find other Pinocchios?"

"To find anything that will make me forget you."

"You know that what I give to others is nothing I take away from you, nothing that belongs to our relationship."

"But Bruce, it's not what you give to others which hurts me, but what you don't give to me, your secrets."

The big log in the fireplace was damp and smoked so heavily that Renate had to open the doors and windows. They both stood shivering in the cold wind that blew from the sea.

Renate said: "I've always loved garden parties."

"Let me tell you my dream. I was listening to music. My body became compressed into a column. At the top of this column grew antennae of science fiction design which threw lassos of blue electric lights in circles. In their centrifugal motion they captured other waves. The waves of the brain? Seeking to contact other vibrations? The radiations of my brain not only designed fever charts but they were neon-lighted and threw off sparks like electric short circuits."

Consolation was a Christian act, not Pan's profession. Bruce could only smile when she could not laugh quickly enough to give her threatening tears time to evaporate. This time they rose to a dangerous water level.

."We can't live our Mexican life here," said Bruce. "Let's get a sailboat and sail around the world. You can paint while we're travelling and I will write my novel. I saw an advertisement that sailboats are very cheap in Holland, and they sell a kind of sailboat which can travel both by sea and by river. I will learn to sail it. You rent the house and meet me in Holland when I am ready."

"I can't imagine you as a captain of a sailboat."

But she felt that perhaps this was the mobility Bruce needed, the fluid, changing, variable way he wanted to live.

He was gone for a month. In his letters he described the old captain who had sold him a sailboat and who was teaching him to run it. The sailboat had a motor too, in case they were becalmed. There was only room for two on the boat so the old captain would not sail with them. But by the time she arrived Bruce felt he could handle it alone.

When she came the captain had waited to greet her and to install her in the small cabin. Then with a salute and a smile he was off.

The boat looked freshly painted and swayed gently by the Dutch pier. Renate loved the lightness of it. She began to unpack, and even set up her painting material.

Bruce called to her. He was tangled in a mass of cords. Renate had not foreseen that she would have to become his assistant. She unknotted cords, pulled at the sails, ran from one end of the boat to the other, watched their swelling, adjusted a hundred clasps and fought for balance against changing winds. Bruce had absorbed little from the Dutch captain. He read directions from a book. He gave orders to Renate in technical language, which she did not understand. By the time they sailed into the first harbor for the night the graceful sailboat seemed more like a wild, unmanageable bronco under their feet.

The constant rocking kept her from sleeping. She felt her hair would wear off completely from the constant friction on her pillow. Duties on board were endless, even when they were not sailing. Renate wanted to return and ask the old captain to help, even if it meant sleeping on deck. But Bruce's pride was offended at this capitulation. At the same time he had never concentrated on any occupation for such long hours and she would find him asleep sometimes under a dangerously swollen sail which would almost tip the boat over.

They decided motoring along rivers might give them more leisure. They folded the sails and used only the motor. When they cast off anchor Renate could not unfasten the thick wet cord at the other end of the boat. Bruce came to help, and as he straddled it to uncoil it from the shore, he fell into the water, and the boat began to drift away from him. He caught up with it only by swimming furiously.

They travelled for a while down the rivers and canals, admiring the soft landscape, the browns and greys so familiar from Dutch paintings. Then the motor sputtered and died. They were in the middle of a swift flowing river, becalmed.

The boat ceased to follow a straight course. Every now and then, like a waltzer, it took a complete turn in the middle of the river.

Its erratic course did not discourage the barges passing by with cargoes and racing for the locks. They travelled at full speed alongside the sailboat, not noticing that Bruce and Renate were rudderless, and that they might at any moment circle in the path of the swift sliding barges.

At one moment the sailboat skirted the shore and Bruce maneuvered it towards the right into a small canal. At this very moment the motor revived and pushed them at full speed under too low a bridge. Scraping this they continued to speed past quiet small houses on the shore. Bruce now could not stop the motor. It had regained its youthful vigor. He stood on the bridge and remembered his western movies. He picked up a coil of rope and lassoed one of the chimneys of a passing house. This stopped the runaway sailboat but drew a crowd around them.

"Crazy Americans," said someone in the crowd.

A policeman came towards them on a bicycle.

"You damaged a historical bridge."

"I didn't know it was historical," said Bruce.

"You will have to appear in court."

That night, like contrabandists, they sailed away (pulled by a tugboat) to a dry dock Bruce had heard of. There he had the boat taken out of the water and loaded on a train.

"What is your plan," asked Renate.

"We'd do better with plenty of room around us, so I thought we'd take the boat to the South of France and sail around the Mediterranean. I'm putting it on the train."

The boat occupied an entire railroad car. They could see it from their carriage when they leaned out of the window. It was exposed to the sun, bottom up. The rigging was dismounted and tied to its sides. The sails looked like folded parachutes. The journey was long and hot, with many stops along the way.

When they reached the South of France it looked to Renate, a painter, exactly like a Dufy poster, all light blue and cream white, sea flags, dresses undulating, brown bodies, music in the cafés, intimate corners for lovers surrounded by oleander bushes, flower vendors at every corner, mimosa, violets, carriages with umbrellas opened over them.

The railroad had taken them to the dry dock with their boat. It was put on wheels.

"We are going to do some spherical sailing," said Bruce. "In spherical sailing, the earth is regarded as a sphere (usually a perfect sphere, though some modern nautical tables allow for its spheroidal shape) and allowance is made for the curvature of its surface."

"Couldn't we do some parallel sailing," asked Renate, who had been reading the same book. "Perhaps we could just sail parallel to the shore. Then we'd never get lost."

The boat was sliding down into the sparkling sea. The men secured the anchor and returned to call for Renate and Bruce and place them upon the deck, and then left them. It was Renate who noticed that it was taking in more than the usual amount of water.

(How could the innocent sailors have known the hot Mediterranean sun would melt the caulking in the boat's bottom during the interminable railroad voyage.)

Bruce turned to the index in the book and read all about

pumping. He pumped for a while and fell asleep. Renate pumped for a while and then felt exhausted and tried to wake Bruce.

"We'll sink if you don't pump out the water, Bruce. Bruce."

"Let it sink," he said and went back to sleep.

Renate wondered if this were a symbolic indication of the pattern their relationship would follow. She went on pumping slowly until Bruce awakened.

The deck was now almost level with the sea. Quietly Renate persuaded Bruce he must put the boat in dry dock and retire from navigation. The motor failing for the last time, Bruce was forced to jump into the sea and tow. As the little boat moved silently towards the dry dock, Renate still pumping slowly, sang a song remembered from childhood:

> *Il était un petit navire*
> *Qui n'avait ja-ja- jamais navigué.*

"From now on our travels will have to be inner voyages. You are only fit to be the captain of Rimbaud's *Bateau Ivre*."

BEHIND RENATE'S HOUSE LAY THE MOUNTAIN. ON TOP OF THE MOUNTAIN a red-tailed missile was planted in its steel cradle, pointing skyward, all set to soar.

The sea had been there once, and left imprints of sea shells and fish skeletons on stone. It had carved deep Venusian caves into the sandstone. The setting sun deposited antique gold on its walls. People on horseback wandered up the mountain. Rabbits, gophers, deer, wild cats and snakes wandered down the mountain and came quite near the house.

Renate's house had glass all along the front. The sea lay below and at times she seemed to be standing against an aluminum sheet. On sunless days, she was profiled against a clouded pond, dull with seaweed trailing scum like sunken marshes.

The sea varied the moods and tones of the house as if both were mobiles in constant mutations.

From Mexico she had brought shawls of unmixed colors, baskets, tin chandeliers, earthenware painted in childish figures, stone pieces like the gods of the Indians.

And then one day at Christmas, the terrified animals ran down from the mountains. Renate saw them running before she heard the sound of crackling wood or saw the flames leaping from hill to hill, across roads, exploding the dry brush, driving people and animals down the canyons and pursuing them satanically down to the very edge of the sea. The fire attacked houses and cars, lit bonfires above the trees, thundered like burning oil wells.

Planes dived and dropped chemicals. Huge tractors cut wide gashes through the forest to cut off the spreading fire. Firefighters climbed up with hose, and vanished into the smoke.

Somewhere, a firebug rejoiced in the spectacle.

Around Renate's house there was no brush, so she hoped to escape the flames. She wrapped herself in a wet blanket and stood on the roof watering it down. But she could feel the heat

27

approaching, and watch its capricious somersaults, unexpected twists and devouring rages.

Bruce helped her for a while and then climbed down. She was still holding the hose and soaking the house when she looked down and saw what first appeared to be the portrait of Bruce walking. The large, life size painting was moving away from the house and two feet showed below the frame, two feet in shoes just below the naked feet of the painting.

The first thing he had asked of her was to stop painting animals and women and to paint a portrait of him. He had shown her the long hairs which grew on his ear lobes and said: "You know that I am Pan, and I want you to paint me as Pan." He had posed nude, in the red-gold afternoon sun of Mexico, always showing the same half-smile, the pleasure loving, non-human smile of Pan. He loved the painting, admired it everyday. It was the god of the household. When they travelled, it was he who had packed it lovingly. He would say: "If any injury came to this painting, it would damage me, something fatal would happen to Pan."

And so today this was Bruce rescuing Bruce, or Bruce rescuing Pan in himself. At first the painting turned its luminous face to her, but as he proceeded down the hill she saw him behind the painting in dungarees and a thick white sweater. She saw a group of firefighters below; she saw the expression on their faces as the painting walked towards them, as they saw first of all a naked Pan with faunish ears, a walking painting with feet, and then the apparition of the same figure dressed in everyday costume upholding its twin, duplicate half-smile, duplicate hands; and they looked startled and puzzled, as if it were superfluous to rescue a mere reproduction of an original.

So Bruce saved Pan, and Renate saved the house but the fire seemed to have finally consumed their relationship.

But after a few days he returned to her.

"After being with you, Renate, other women seem like baby foods after being on heroin."

He had spent the time searching for a remedy for their relationship.

"It is my secrecy which makes you unhappy, my evasions, my silences. And so I have found a solution. Whenever you get desperate with my mysteries, my ambiguities, here is a set of Chinese puzzle boxes. You have always said that I was myself a Chinese puzzle box. When you are in the mood and I baffle your love of confidences, your love of openness, your love of sharing experiences, then open one of the boxes. And in it you will find a story, a story about me and my life. Do you like this idea? Do you think it will help us to live together?"

Renate laughed and accepted. She took the armful of boxes and laid them away on the top shelf of a closet.

The time came again, when she felt she did not possess a love; that a love which was mute, elusive, and vague was not really a love. So she brought down the Chinese boxes, scattered them on the table, picked one at random as a man plays roulette, and began with patience to slide the polished slats. The beige wood painted with abstract designs of dark brown created a new design each time which did not guide her through the baffling labyrinth of panels and slats. But finally after long shuffling, sliding, turning, she found the compartment and pulled out a tightly folded sheet.

She read: "When I first met Ken I was seventeen. He was only a year older but because his father had been a missionary in China and he had been born there, he possessed a maturity I did not have. He very soon dominated my life. He had no connection with the daily world, only with dreams and fantasies. I stopped swimming, surf-boarding, mountain climbing, gave up my other friends to be taken wholly into his magic world. What imprisoned me, restricted me had no power over him. He was not even aware of jobs, careers, studies, parents, duties, ties or responsibilities of any kind. He confessed that he was helped by opium. But I refused to take it with him. He admitted that since his return from China, unknown to his father, he had been taking too much of it. Every now and then he would pass out. I would

29

come to his room and find him deeply asleep, but with a pinched nose, and unhealthy pallor. I would return a day later and he would still be asleep. He knew the opium was bad for him but he could not stop. I tried to help him. I became very firm. I said if he did not begin to work on his film project which we were going to carry out together, I would leave him. This frightened him. I was his only friend. We took a trip to Mexico together. There I thought he was cured. We were working on our film and he took such pleasure in photographing me and in inventing situations. One night I stayed out later than usual at a native wedding. He had pleaded fatigue and had returned to the hotel. When I returned, he was in that deep sleep I could tell apart from normal sleep. He was still sleeping the next day. I did not like his color. He had the ivory wax color of death. I called the village doctor. He took one look at him and said: 'He's had too much opium. I'm not a doctor for drug addicts. He may never wake up.' I had heard that in such cases if he could wake up enough to smoke a pipe he would come to. I prepared a pipe exactly as I had seen him do it. I was frightened. His breathing was so feeble I could hardly hear it at times. But I could not wake him up sufficiently to make him smoke. Deserted by the doctor, all alone in the Mexican desert, I wondered how to save him. I began to remember the time I had been closest to death. I was swimming and I had been carried too far out by a riptide. I stayed too long in the water. I did not remember being rescued, but I did remember the lifeguard who gave me mouth to mouth respiration. Mouth to mouth respiration! I took Ken's pipe and I smoked, absorbing and holding the smoke and then I leaned over, opened his lips and blew the smoke into his lungs several times, until he finally breathed deeply again and opened his eyes. That was the beginning . . ."

Renate sat in the sunlight which, reflected from the sea below, made the ceiling and walls dissolve in waves of lights and shadows. The stripes on walls and on the table seemed to place her inside a Chinese box compartment, too, as a figure in Bruce's past. When he returned she was still sitting there with the puzzle box open on her knees. She received him with tenderness and with a silence which did not resemble his, for his eyes when he was silent resembled the cool colorless spray of fountains, whereas her eyes showered him with gold specks like those which fell from the fireworks in Mexico on the night they had felt welded like twins.

"You say I only love myself," he had said then, "that I love Pan, and Pan is me; but you, why have you only painted women?"

Weeks passed before she felt the need to open another box. Bruce was acting in a film. His director took him fishing. She did not like fishing any more than she liked the hunting of birds. She was alone for three days. During those three days she thought that her imagination had created the image of a greater union between Bruce and young men than he had with her, but now she was not sure. She felt that Ken had not been able to win him to his world of opium. She felt the isolation of Ken. She felt the need to know Bruce intimately even if it was not today's Bruce she was discovering but yesterday's.

The second box took longer to open. She had made a pyramid of them, and then opened the one at the top. She read:

"In Mexico Ken and I found many beautiful boys. We hired them for a few pesos. We taught them the pleasures of whipping each other. Ken's knowledge of the art was incredible. He was a virtuoso in gradations. We started with gentle lashings and ended with wounding bamboo. The ritual we preferred was going out into the woods at dawn, cutting down selected branches of bamboo and playing at pursuing and capturing the victims. Somehow or other one morning we became separated. I was left alone with the youngest boy. I had promised him he could beat me this time. He kept touching my skin, amazed at the whiteness, and expressing what a pleasure it would be to mark it up. He dug his nails into my arm. When we got to the clearing and cut down the branches, I was roused by the boy's anticipation of pleasure and I turned upon him and beat him. We did not notice some peasants who were walking to work. They spotted us first and silently surrounded us. They were at first amazed by the spectacle of two naked boys, and then they were angry. I was holding the bamboo. I saw them standing in a circle looking at me. All their eyes looked fiercely angry. I panicked and said the first thing which came to my mind, out of fear: 'I'm beating him because he stole my watch.' The boy was put in jail for three years. As they took him away he shouted at me: 'When I come out I will kill you!' I had to leave Mexico."

Renate took the pages, folded them as tightly as they had been folded to fit into the compartment, pushed them into the opening, and slipped the various slats back into place, as if she would bury the story forever. She walked down the hill with the box. She stood on the edge of the rock, and threw it in a wide, high arc, into the sea. Then she returned home, placed the pyramid of boxes inside the fireplace and set fire to them.

RENATE GATHERED TOGETHER ALL THE LINEN OF THE HOUSE STAINED
with marks of love, dreams, nightmares, tears and kisses and quarrels, the mists that rise from bodies touching, the fogs of breathing, the dried tears, and took it to the laundromat at the foot
of the hill.

The man who ran it mystified her. He was tall, dark-skinned,
dark-eyed. He wore a red shirt which set off his foreign hand-
someness. But it was not this which made his presence there
unexpected. It was the pride of his carriage, and his delicate way
of handling the laundry. He greeted Renate with colorful mod-
ulations of a voice trained to charm. He bowed as he greeted
her. His hands were long-fingered, deft.

He folded the dry sheets as if he were handling lace tablecloths. He was aloof, polite, as if laundry were a country gentleman's natural occupation. He took money as if it were a bouquet.
He returned change as if it were a glass of champagne.

He never commented on the weather, as if it were a plebeian
interest. He piled up the laundry as if he were merely checking
the contents of his own home's closets. He was proud and gracious. He pretended not to see the women who came in hair
curlers, like a high born valet who overlooks his master's occasional lapse in manners.

For Renate he had a full smile. His teeth were strong and
even but for one milk tooth which gave his smile a touch of humor.

Renate also handled her bundle of laundry as if it were pastry
from a fashionable shop.

The rhythm of the machines became like the opening notes
of an orchestra at a ball. She never mentioned the weather either,
as if they both understood weather was a mere background to
more important themes. They agreed that if human beings had
to attend to soiled laundry, they had been given, at the same time,
a faculty for detaching themselves, not noticing, or forgetting cer-

tain duties and focusing on how to enhance, heighten, add charm to daily living.

Renate would tell him about each visitor who had come to see her, describe each costume, each character, each conversation, and then hand over the bundle as if it were the discarded costumes which had to be re-glamorized for the next party. While she talked they both handled the guest towels from Woolworth's as if they were lace tablecloths from Brussels.

He looked over the bundles lined up on the shelf and ready to be called for as if he were choosing a painting in an art exhibition and said: "I always recognize yours by its vivid colors."

As his brown, fine-bred hand rested on the blue paper around the package, she noticed for the first time a signet ring on his finger. It was a gold coat-of-arms.

She bent over it to examine the symbols. The ring was divided into four sections. On one was engraved a lion's head, on the second a small castle, on the third a four-leaf clover, and on the fourth a Maltese cross.

"But I have seen this design somewhere," said Renate. "Could it have been on one of the shields on one of the statues in a Vienna park?"

"Yes, it could have been. I have some ancestors there. My family has a castle forty miles from Vienna. My parents still live there. The coat-of-arms is that of Count Osterling."

He brought out his wallet. Instead of photographs of round-faced babies she saw a turreted castle. Two dignified old people stood on the terrace. The man wore a beard. The woman carried an umbrella. One could see lace around her throat. Her hand rested on the head of a small boy.

"That is me."

Renate did not want to ask: and how did you come here, what are you doing here when you could be opening bottles of old vintage wine from your own property, sitting at beautiful dining tables and being waited on?

"After the war we were land poor. I felt our whole life growing static and difficult. Tradition prevented me from working at any job. I came to America. I went to Chicago. I was only seventeen and it was all new and elating. I felt like a pioneer. I liked forgetting the past and being able to work without feeling I was humiliating a whole set of relatives. I did all kinds of jobs. I liked the freedom of it. Then I met the Rhinegold Beauty Queen that year. She was unbelievably beautiful. I married her. I did not even know what her father did. Later I found out he owned a chain of laundromats. He put me to work as an inspector. At first we travelled a lot, but when he died we wanted to stay in one place and raise children. So we came here."

"You never went home again?"

"We did once, but my wife did not like it. She thought the castle was sad. She was cold, and the plumbing was not efficient. She didn't like so much politeness, motheaten brocades, yellowed silks, dust on the wine bottles."

Count Laundromat, she called him, as she watched the gold signet ring with the family coat-of-arms flashing through detergents.

An enormous woman appeared through the back door and called out to him. She was as tall and as wide as Mae West. The beautiful eyes, features and hair were deeply imbedded in cushions of flesh like a jewel in a feather bedspread.

"My wife," he said, to Renate, and to her he said: "This is a neighbor who once lived in Vienna."

Then he took up her bundle of laundry and carried it to the car, opened the door, fitted it in the seat with care that no piece should be caught when the door closed, as if it were the lacy edge of a petticoat.

From the day he told her the story of his title, the smell of kitchen soap, of wet linen, wet wool, detergents, became confused in Renate's nostrils with the smell of an antique cabinet she had once opened in a shop in Vienna.

The inside of the drawers were lined with brocade which was glued to the wood and which retained the smell of sandalwood. The past was like those old-fashioned sachet bags filled with herbs and flowers which penetrate the clothes and cling to them.

Everytime she visited Count Laundromat, the perfumes of the antique cabinet enveloped her, the smell of the rose petals her mother kept in a small music box, the smell of highly polished sandalwood of her sewing table, the vanilla of Viennese pastry, the pungent spices, the tobacco from her father's pipe, all these overpowered the detergents.

IN THE SMALL TOWNS OF CALIFORNIA THE OCCASIONAL ABSENCE OF inhabitants, or animation, can give the place the air of a still life painting. Thus it appeared for a moment in the eyes of a woman standing in the center of an empty lot. No cars passed, no light shone, no one walked, no windows blinked, no dogs barked, no children crossed the street.

The place had a soft name: Downey. It suggested the sensation of downy hairs on downy skins. But Downey was not like its name. It was symmetrical, tidy, monotonous. One house could not be distinguished from another, and gaping open garages exposed what was once concealed in attics; broken bicycles, old newspapers, old trunks, empty bottles.

The woman who was standing in the empty lot had blurred her feminine contours in slacks, and a big loose sweater. But her blonde hair was round and puffed like the hair of a doll.

She stood motionless and became, for a moment, part of the still life until a station wagon arrived and friends waved at her as they slowed down in front of her. She ran swiftly towards them and helped them open the back of the car and unload paintings and easels which they all carried to the empty lot.

Then the woman in slacks became intensely active, placing and turning the paintings at an angle where the sunlight would illumine rather than consume them.

The paintings were all in sharp contrast to the attenuated colors of Downey. Deep nocturnal blues and greens and purples, all the velvet tones of the night.

Cars began to stop and people came to look.

One visitor said: "These trees have no shadows."

Another visitor said: "The faces have no wrinkles. They do not look real."

The crowd that had gathered was the same one who came to the empty lot at Christmas to buy Christmas trees, or in the summer to buy strawberries from the Japanese gardeners.

"I have never seen a sea like this," said another spectator.

The woman in slacks laughed and said: "A painting should take you to a place you have never seen before. You don't always want to look at the same tree, the same sea, the same face every day, do you?"

But that was exactly what the inhabitants of Downey wanted to do. They did not want to uproot themselves. They were looking for duplicates of Downey, a portrait of their grandmother, and of their children.

The painter laughed. They liked her laughter. They ventured to buy a few of the smaller paintings, as if in diminutive sizes they might not be so dangerous or change the climate of their living-room.

"I'm helping you to tell your house apart from your neighbor's," said the painter.

There was no wind. Between visitors the painter and her friends sat on stools and smoked and talked among themselves. But one capricious, solitary puff of wind lifted a strand of blonde hair away from the painter's face and revealed a strand of dark hair under the mesh of the wig. But no one noticed or commented on it.

The light grew dim. The painter and her friends packed the remaining paintings and drove away.

Back at her house by the sea, the painter stacked her paintings against the wall. She went into her bedroom. When she came out again the wig was gone, her long black hair fell over her shoulders, and she wore a Mexican cotton dress in all the soft colors of a rainbow.

It was Renate. The blonde wig lay on the bed, with the slacks and the big sweater. And now she also had to make the paintings look like her own art work again, which meant restituting to them the fantasmagorical figures of her night dreams. The plain landscapes, the plain seascapes, the plain figures were all transformed to what they were before the Downey exhibit. The figures undulated, became bells, the bells rang over the ocean, the trees waved in cadences, the sinuosities of the clouds were like the scarves of

38

Arab or Hindu women, veiling the storms. Animals never seen before, descendents of the unicorn, offered their heads to be cajoled. The vegetative patience of flowers was depicted like a group of twittering nuns, and it was the animals who had the eyes of crystal gazers while people's eyes seemed made of stalactites. Explosions of the myth, talkative garrulous streets, debauched winds, oracular moods of the sands, stasis of the rocks, attrition of stones, acerose of leaves, excresence of hours, sibylline women with a faculty for osmosis, adolescence like cactus, the corrugations of age, the ulcerations of love, people seeking to live two lives with one heart, inseparable twins.

She restored to the empty landscapes all the mythological figures of her dreams, thinking of Rousseau's words in answer to the question: "Why did you paint a couch in the middle of the jungle?" And he had said: "Because one has a right to paint one's dreams."

Renate was painting a canal of Venice, shimmering like an unrolled bolt of changeable lamé silver and gold, and the shadow of a gondolier upon the water, the one seen by Byron or by Georges Sand. But the gondola in reality was passing by and through the shadow with a gondolier dressed in work clothes, not in his nautical finery. And what he was transporting was not a pair of entranced lovers but a couch, quite obviously newly covered with fresh and vivid red brocade. To be delivered speedily to some occupied palace, occupied by a new enemy, the renovators. The second gondolier, while waiting to help carry the couch to its owner, was resting upon it, at ease, and had fallen asleep.

Renate was laughing. She finished the painting with the face of a cat looking through a heavily barred window.

When she was a child she felt that she had been born in the world to rescue all the animals. She was concerned with the bondage and slavery of animals, the donkey on the treadmills in Egypt, the cattle traveling in trains, chickens tied together by the legs, rabbits being shot in the forest, dogs on leashes, kittens left starving on the sidewalks. She made several attempts to rescue them. She cut the strings around the chicken's legs and they scattered all over the market place. She opened all the cages she could find and let the birds fly out. She opened field gates and let the cattle wander.

It was only when she reached the age of fourteen that she realized the hopelessness of her task. Cruelty extended too far. She could never hope to extinguish it. It stretched from the peaks of Peru and the jungle of Africa to Arcadia, California, where the inhabitants protested against the wild peacocks who were wandering in the neighborhood and had them arrested.

So Renate began to paint the friendship of women and animals. She painted a luminous woman lying peacefully beside a panther, a woman with blue-tinted flesh floating on the opening wing of a swan, a woman with eyes like the eyes of her Siamese cat, a woman tenderly holding a turtle.

This turtle was so small that Renate had to use a magnifying glass to study its eyes. She was quite startled when she found herself facing the cold, malevolent glance of the turtle. Renate did not believe in the malevolence of animals. She had thought first of imprisoned animals; then of free animals; and finally of women and animals living in harmony.

She was now painting Raven, a girl with very long black hair and a pale skin who owned a raven, and whose wish for a raven had been born so early in her life that she could not remember how it had been born, whether from Edgar Allan Poe's poem, or from a small engraving she still carried about as others carry photographs of their children.

She had always considered herself too gentle, too pliant. This dream of a fierce raven seemed to balance elements of her being.

"His black wings, his sharp beak, his strong claws completed me, added something I lacked, added the element of darkness," she told Renate.

She searched for a raven and grew concerned when she heard that they were nearly exterminated in the United States.

She went to visit ravens at the zoo. She read that they had once been an object of veneration and superstition. Symbol of the night, of the dark side of our being? She noticed too that they were intelligent and mischievous. They learned to articulate words in a hoarse, cracked bass voice.

Once in San Francisco she picked up a newspaper and there was an advertisement by a rich eccentric old lady who had collected birds and animals and was forced to move back to Europe. She had a raven for sale.

Raven rushed to see her and met her raven there. She made a down payment and asked the old lady to hold him for her until she found a proper home for him. But before she was quite ready, she received a telegram: "Raven arriving by T.W.A. Airline Flight 6 at 8 p.m. today."

The image of her raven flying in a box from San Francisco startled Raven. She had somehow expected him to fly over on his own power.

When she found him in his box at the airport he seemed crestfallen and humiliated. His wings were held close to his body as if the flight had handicapped him forever. He looked angrily at the plane as an unworthy rival. He cackled and made harsh angry sounds. Raven took him home.

She had to buy a huge cage. But she was happy. She felt she had fulfilled a long dream, she felt complete in herself. In the raven lay some mute, unflying part of herself which would now become visible, audible and in flight. His wings, so wide open and powerful, became her wings. His blackness became her blackness. And the child in Raven who had been too gentle, too docile, now felt liberated of this meek image, felt that the raven had become a part of her she wanted to express, a stronger, darker, more independent self. His irony, his mockery, his fierceness suited her. They were extensions of a Raven who might have otherwise become selfless, self-effacing. So Raven sat on the red couch, and her raven wandered through the room, the raven of legends, ravenous, ravishing, raper, rapacious. But Raven loved him in all his moods.

His black feathers full of dark blue lustre, his eyes so sharp, his claws curling twice around the bars of his cage, he stared at Renate who was staring at him, a black rayless stare.

Raven loosened the chain. Renate expected him to perch on Raven's hair or shoulders. She wanted to see hair and wings entangled. But Raven and the bird displayed no intimacy. He pecked with his long beak at Raven's toes. His hoarse vague sounds, like a man clearing his throat after smoking, filled the room as he flew from his perch with the speed of wind.

The young men who visited Raven considered the bird a menace, a challenge, a rival, a test of their courage, of their masculinity. They could not court her, dream of her, in front of him. They wanted to provoke him and drive him away, as if in some obscure way he guarded Raven from intimacy with them. He was an obstacle, an alien part of her, ruling a realm they did not want to know. He stared at their eyes as if meditating an attack.

Raven controlled him like a lion tamer, shook a folded newspaper to drive him back into his cage, but Renate could see she enjoyed his angry retreats.

Raven said: "After I tamed him, I let him run free in the apartment. I wanted to know if he really loved me, if he would stay with me. So I opened the window and he flew out to the roof of the house next door. He explored the gutters, pecked at some stray leaves, and flew back to me. From then on I knew I was as necessary to him as he was to me."

The raven trod gingerly between delicate furniture, vases, statuettes and brocades. But when he spread his wings and shook them, tremulous with rhythm and vibrations, one could hear the wind from the mountains where ravens like to live, and one marvelled that he submitted to captivity.

How intently he looked at Raven, her hair and eyebrows matching his wings but seeming blacker by contrast with her moonlit skin.

Posing for Renate, Raven contemplated her painting of Our Lady of the Beast. In the late afternoon light a luminous naked woman reclines beside a panther. The face of the panther shines more brightly with a phosphorescent light. They are the Beauty and the Beast after a long marriage, both equally beautiful. But later, when it grew dark, it was the face and body of the woman which began to shine with a gold phosphorescence and the panther grew darker and more shadowy. It disappeared finally into the night, leaving on the black canvas only the stare of its golden eyes. They had exchanged souls.

Renate painted Raven standing nude in front of a mirror. Her back was covered with her abundant, undulating black hair. Her reflection in the mirror was smaller, the skin a shade paler, her eyebrows and eyelashes touched with coal dust. The raven was pecking at the hem of her lace scarf, with his wings closed as if the girl had become more powerful than the raven. The quality of night, mystery and hidden violence had been absorbed by her.

And the raven, sitting at her feet with folded wings, had he absorbed her timidity?

WHILE DRIVING ALONG PACIFIC PALISADES, RENATE HAD STOPPED several times to offer a lift to an old man with his arm in a sling. He was going to get his arm treated nearby and, very slowly, he unravelled his story to her.

He lived in Malibu, the place by the sea which the Indians called the Humped Mountain, and which in French, if you sang it, sounded like Evil Owl—*Mal Hibou,* Malibu.

When he was a young man he became a lifeguard at Will Rogers' beach. He sat on a chair twelve feet high and studied the moods of the sea. He had no need of weather bureaus. He knew by every undulation, every contortion, every flourish and flounce of the waves, the sea's exact mood and whether it would be treacherous for the swimmers, or tender and mocking. He knew the omens of the clouds, read the future in their colors and density. He knew the topography of the sand covered by the sea as if he had mapped its depths. From where he sat the cries of the gulls, of children and bathers all fused together and made a sound he liked, *musique concréte.* He had never been concerned with words.

He knew the entire coast, from Will Rogers' beach to where Malibu became wild and solitary.

He married and had children, but he was restless in the house. The static walls irked him. He did not like the smell of enclosure, of cooking, of wax, nor the sound of the vacuum cleaner. He missed the wind's flurries, and the spicy smells of the seashore. He felt entombed by the stillness of objects, the unchanging landscapes in frames. And the torrent of words spoken by his wife and children did not give him the stinging, whipping sense of aliveness he felt at the beach.

He returned to his old job as a lifeguard. But each evening he stayed longer at the beach. He liked it best when it was deserted, and when he would start walking homeward along the coast. He discovered the treasures of the sea which lay in the rock

44

crevices, either thrown there by storms, or growing there. The humid, never-withering sea-lemon, the sea-lilies which did not close at night, the sea-lentils tied to giant serpentine string beans, sea-liquor brine, sea-lyme grass, sea-moss, sea-cucumbers. He never knew the sea had such a lavish garden—sea-plumes, sea-grapes, sea-lace, sea-lungs. In the summer he began to stay on after dark. He learned skin diving and stole crabs and lobsters people trapped. He cooked his dinner on the beach. He came home rarely.

The rocks were continually filled with surprises from shipwrecks, and the nights with sounds which the regular rhythm of the sea orchestrated. The wind flung itself between the rocks, dishevelled, wrestled with the waves, until one of them expired. The sky put on its own evanescent spectacles, a pivoting stage, fugitive curtains, decors for ballets, floating icebergs, unrolled bolts of chiffon, gold and pearl necklaces, marabous of oyster white, scarves of Indian saris, flying feathers, shorn lambs, geometric architecture in snows and cotton. His theater was the clouds, where no spectacle repeated itself.

On land he was a foreigner. Land for him was stasis, and it pulled him into immobility, which was his image of death.

One night he slept in one of the caves. He thought to himself: Now I am a merman.

He passed the time detecting mild sea-quakes, he made friends with the sea-lark, he collected sea-palms and made a rug of them for his cave. But some element was missing. The friendship of the sea-gulls was too ephemeral. Their visits were too short. They were always impatient to be off in space.

One night he walked on to the end of a natural rock jetty and came upon a shoal of seals. They swam, dived, clowned, but always crawled back to the rocks to have their young ones there. They kissed, barked, leaped, danced on their partly fused hind limbs. Their black eyes were like mirrors reflecting sea and sky, but the ogival shape of their eyelids gave them an air of compassion, almost as if they would weep with sympathy. Their tails were of little use except for swimming but they liked to shake

45

their webbed flipper-like limbs as if they were about to fly. Their fur shone like onyx, with dark blue shadows under the fins.

They greeted the man with cries of joy. By this time he was an old man. The sea had wrinkled his face so intricately, it was a surprise when his smile scattered the lines to shine through, like a beautiful glossy fish darting out of a fishing net.

The old man fed the seals, he settled near them in a cave, cooked his dinner, and rolled over and fell asleep with a new feeling of companionship.

One night several men came. They wanted to catch the seals for a display in a pool in front of their restaurant. A publicity stunt which attracted the children. But the pool was small, it was surrounded by barbed wire and the old man did not want this to happen to his seals. So he warned them by an imitation of their cry and bark, and they dove quickly into the sea. By the time the men reached the end of the jetty the seals were gone. From then on the old man felt he was their guardian. No one could get through at night without walking through his bedroom. In spite of the tap-dancing of the waves, and the siren calls of the wind, the old man would hear the dangerous visitors and always had time to warn the seals in their own language.

The old man discovered the seal's names. They answered to Hilarious, Ebenezer, Ambrosius, Eulalee and Adolfo. But there was one seal whose name he did not know, who was too old when they first met. The old man did not have the courage to try out names on him, to see which one he answered to, for the seal could hardly move and it would have humiliated him.

One severe winter the old man's children began to worry about him, as he was growing old and rheumatic. One rainy day they came and forced him into their car, and took him to their home and fixed him up a bedroom.

The first night he slept on a bed, he fell off and broke his arm. As soon as his arm was well again he returned to the cave.

One night when he felt minor quakes were taking place in the area of his heart, he thought he was going to die, so he tried to crawl nearer to the seals, into the crevices where they slept. But they gently, compassionately, nosed him out of the place.

By then he resembled them so much, with his mustache, his rough oval eyebrows, his drooping eyelids, and his barking cough, that he thought they would help him to slide down the rocks and be buried at sea, like a true seal.

WHEN RENATE DID NOT SELL ENOUGH PAINTINGS SHE WORKED AS A hostess at Paradise Inn. The nightclub, built of rocks and wood, stood high on a rock above the beach. Palm trees and cactus gave it a semblance of tropical softness which was belied by the sharpness of the wind. It was more pleasurable to sit inside near the big fire in the fireplace, and to contemplate the sea through the enormous windows.

Renate wore a purple dress she had made herself and so it did not have the shapelessness of fashion but followed the natural contours of her body like a second skin.

She was always in movement, throwing her long black hair back away from her face, moving forward to greet the visitors, and when she turned her face towards the bar it seemed as if she set the whole glittering mechanism in motion to satisfy hunger and thirst.

She was so gracious in her gestures of welcome that the diners often stopped talking and drinking to watch her, as if she were the spectacle they had come to see. The bar man looked at her while he shook his potions, the old chef looked at her over his charcoal pit, the musicians sang for her, looked at her over the black wings of the piano, and one thought of the French word for hostess, *entraîneuse*, which meant to pull, to magnetize, to lure in her wake.

Eat, drink, talk, she seemed to whisper as she placed the menu into the visitor's hand, as if she were giving them the secret to all delights, and often they moved aside to make room and said: "Renate, sit down, have a drink with us."

Animator, bringing animation to silent tables, staying long enough to light the candles.

They arrived in disparate costumes, formal and informal, summer coats, furs, gloves, sport shirts, Hawaiian shirts, *Harper's Bazaar* plumes, racing-car goggles, motorcycle helmets, dancing pumps, or leather boots. They arrived heavily made up, with false eyelashes, wigs, or unkempt, ungroomed. No one was surprised. It was the movie colony, at work on films. It looked as if they had snatched a few items from the costume department: beards, gangster's raincoats, the star's false jewels. It matched the jumbled styles of their homes, imitations of the styles of other countries which, bereft of their natural atmosphere, looked like stage sets.

Nothing seemed to belong to them organically, to be stamped with their own identity, but no one seemed to expect that. Even the painters and writers wore disguises which outdid Venetian masked balls. The beards of men shipwrecked for years on desert islands, the unmatched clothes from thrift shops, the girls with hair uncombed, and black cotton stockings, and eyes painted a tubercular violet. In this costume they meant to convey a break with conventions, with the stylish mannequins in Beverly Hills shop windows, but it created the impression of merely another uniform, which they bore self-consciously, and it did not portray freedom, nonchalance. They wore them stiffly, as if on display, like extras for a Bohemian scene, proclaiming: look at me.

All of them were impatient to drink the dissolvent remedy which would loosen the disguise, disintegrate the self-conscious shell, to drink until the lower depths of their nature would rise to the surface in sodden debris, brash words, acid angers, to shatter the mannequins they stifled in, to shatter the disguises.

"Renate," they called, not because they were hungry or thirsty, but because she knew who she was, and as she knew who she was, she might also be able to identify them, with a smile and a word, just as with a smile and a word she had said to Bruce: "You are a poet."

There was food on the table, and the glasses were full, but who was at the table? Would Renate know? They were at sea, and Renate was more than a woman, she was a compass. What confused them did not confuse her. If she did not answer their distress signals, if she left them stranded in the vacuum they lived in, then to assert their existence they would have to begin a quarrel with someone, anyone.

The features became muddied, the façades collapsed. When a glass broke, Renate appeared as if this were a signal of danger, the start of a drama, as if the restaurant had become a ship at sea, and they all floundered on waves of anger. Strangers were flung together and collided in tidal waves of alcohol, in incoherent quarrels.

I am a star, I am a director, I am a cameraman, I am married, I have two children, I have discovered oil, I have built a house, I have written a script, I won the Oscar, I bought a horse, I rented my ranch, I started the fashion of boar hunting, I am having an exhibition, I am sailing to Acapulco.

But none of these facts had the full-bodied power Renate had when she said: "I am a painter."

Her painting had been born from within just as her son had been, organic, part of her flesh, whereas for the desperate anonymous, they were adopted accidental children, not truly their own, and they were not certain of paternity or reality.

There was one more personage who was not foundering in anonymity like a pilot in weightless space, and that was Leontine who was singing by the piano.

Her hair was cut in a boyish style with bangs over her eyes. It had been dipped in a red glow. Her skin was of a creamy chocolate, her eyes black and highly polished. Her fingers were long and sensitive when she touched her long neck, to feel where the voice came from, as if to coax it pure, and out it came honeyed and heavy, warming, tender, at times like silk, at other times like zephyr wool on the skin.

She wore a long jersey swathe striped black and white, with a turtle neck which accentuated the Ubangi length of her neck, and black tights which gave her the air of a medieval page.

When she finished her song, she rushed to embrace Renate: "You didn't recognize me! I'm Leontine!"

"You've changed so much!" said Renate.

"Do you remember the first time we met?"

"Of course I remember. It was at Canada Lee's New Year's

party. You were fifteen years old. You had a humorous, turned up nose . . . ."

"I changed that, for the photographers," said Leontine.

"I remember you danced Haitian dances. It was my first year in America. I did not feel at home yet. It was my first meeting with the dead pan faces of New York City, a Greek play with masks, and all the dead pans seemed to say: 'We don't know you. We don't see you. We don't like you.' This New Year's party was my first one in New York, and when Canada Lee greeted me at the door with his warm melting voice and his joyous smile and said: 'Come in, hang up your coat,' as if he meant it and were addressing me personally, I wept. It was my first personal, intimate, friendly welcome. And then you came and put your arms around me, and took me to meet your father. But he was formal and impressive, as if carved of wood. He had all the Haitian dignity and formality. His stiff silver-gray hair was cut short like the bristle of a hard brush. Immediately he began to tell me a story I never forgot."

"It was always the same story," said Leontine. "About his youth in Haiti and his revolutionary activities, how he was sentenced to life imprisonment and sent to Guiana. How he was tied by a chain to another prisoner."

"The unendurable heat, the sadism of the guards. The same place and the same conditions as for Dreyfus. He was only seventeen and condemned for life. I forgot how they managed to escape."

"They worked at it for two years. They planned well, and found themselves in the jungle, miles from the sea where a boat with friends awaited them. They fed on fruit, and slept in caves, or inside dead trees. They were bitten by insects. The chain binding their arms made walking difficult. They had no way to cut the chain. It was too heavy to wear down by scraping against a stone. On the third day my father's companion drank polluted water and on the fourth day he died. And my father was chained to a dead man."

"At this point I told your father I did not want to hear any

51

more. His story and the gaiety of the New Year's party all around us was too violent a contrast. I covered my ears. The room was filled with laughter and jazz dancing. The New Year was being greeted with firecrackers and shouts and kisses. Your father sat impervious, unmoved by all the agitation and continued his story. How he had freed himself by cutting the arm off at the shoulder with a small knife. But he had to carry the dead arm all the way to the boat."

"Covered with ants," said Leontine. "I'm sorry if I sound callous, Renate, but my father told this story so many times that I couldn't feel any emotion any more."

"You were dancing Haitian dances. Don't you dance any more?"

"I was too lazy to be a dancer. I hated rehearsals. I took up singing instead, which came naturally to me. It didn't require so much discipline."

"And what happened to all the wishes you made? You wanted a life like Josephine Baker's. You wanted to live in France, and marry a French count and have a palace in Marrakesh."

"I did travel with Catherine Dunham. I did get to France, and I did find my French count. He was not handsome, but he was tall and blond. He thought I was not intelligent and so he invented a language for me, half-baby-talk, half monkey-chatter, which he thought I would understand better. He had a sadistic sense of humor. Once he called for me at the Hotel de Crillon in an Arab costume, a poor soiled one, as if he had slept in it for weeks. The manager was entertaining Arab royalty. The secret service men wanted to arrest him. Then they found out he was the son of a deputy. Another time he rented a beautiful apartment for me but gave me no furniture. Then he gave a party for me. We entertained in leotards and jewelry. The fabulous jewelry he had "borrowed" from his mother who alerted the police. He never told me where it came from and I wore it at the night club and the same secret service men came to my dressingroom. He had to explain where it came from. Another time we sat for hours in a crowded café and insulted each other. People who were concerned over the racial equality were so shocked by what he said they wanted to interfere, until they heard what I was saying to him. Another time he told me to wear my loveliest dress, we were going to Maxim's. He left me sitting at our table and went to the coat room to leave his overcoat. He was wearing the jacket of his formal suit over leotards. He insisted on taking me out to dance. Because his father was a deputy, no one interfered with him. Another time I had a jealous tantrum at the Ritz bar, and I began to break glasses. My Count calmly called the headwaiter and said: "Bring me a tray with a dozen of your best glasses. If Madame feels like breaking glasses she must have the best." This embarrassed me so much I left the place. He always had the upper hand; he always won and I enjoyed that. He spread the rumor that I had a neurotic fear of automobiles and made me go about in a horse and carriage, and insisted I ride in it dressed in jeans. That was the time a man stopped the carriage and said to me: "You must be Leontine. I am Cocteau." With my Count, it was not so much a physical fascination as a mental one. We were both absurd. No, he never did marry me, and I never did live in a palace in Marrakesh, but he made me laugh for three and a half years."

"I remember your mother too," said Renate.

"She worked in a factory stuffing woolly animals with sawdust. She smuggled out the best ones for you, bears, camels, donkeys. Your mother was very worried about your infatuation for your cousin, who was much whiter than you. She was afraid he would take advantage of you and then not marry you. She asked me to find out how things were, and I didn't want to pry. So I invented a charade in which you had to act a woman being made love to, and the cooing, dove sounds you made were so realistic I knew your mother's fears were justified."

"I remember the day I came to get you to go to the beach. I found you bathing in tea, you were ashamed of being so white."

"I also remember the day you mentioned a Haitian national party you were going to and I said I would love to come, too, and you looked at me wistfully and said: 'Renate, white people are not invited.'"

Leontine laughed, and her long gold earrings tinkled, and her bracelets tinkled, and her long chain of beads, and the spotlight found her lighting up her eyes and smile. She went back to the piano to sing for Renate, and Renate could find no trace of the little girl with tight curls and a turned up nose who played in the streets of Brooklyn with lions, kangaroos and monkeys stuffed and sewn by her mother in a nearby factory which looked like a prison.

Henri the chef was the adopted son of the famous Escoffier. No one knew why he had settled in Paradise Inn, in a kitchen where his historic copper pans and kettles looked like those of a giant. He had hung them all on the wall and kept the copper shining like mirrors in which he could read of his past splendors and victories.

Henri was tall, but with his chef's bonnet he seemed to touch the ceiling. He was also sumptuously upholstered by rich eating, and when he moved between the carving board and the stove, he had to pull in his vast stomach.

When he had finished cooking, the guests wanted to hear his anecdotes. Late in the evening he would bring small roses to the ladies and a profusion of biographical stories.

All the people he had cooked for bore famous names, from Queen Victoria to Diamond Jim Brady. He described them in a décor of crystal chandeliers, candlelight, lace tablecloths, attended by armies of assistants. He recalled the exact compliments he had received from kings, famous actors, society women, and later, from tycoons, gangsters and business dictators.

He had been a child prodigy in the kitchen, later a dictator ruling over his own culinary inventions.

His monumental figure and red face seemed composed of all the delicacies he had cooked, an attrition of sauces, flavors, spices and wines.

All the stories he served with the dishes were of ancient vintage. He had invented the Crêpe Suzette for Prince Edward, the charcoal broiled steak for Diamond Jim Brady.

Dazzled by the past, he seemed near-sighted about present celebrities. Perhaps he felt that in the past he had played a major role, and that the visitors who came now were witnessing his ageing. At one time his dinners could influence the atmosphere of a political discussion and affect history; they could decide the course of a love affair.

Perhaps he felt reluctant to admit that among today's diners there might be one future celebrity who might usher in an equally brilliant era but an era he would not be there to feed.

As he was past eighty, many of his anecdotes ended in funeral orations. Some of his flambées, accompanied by a list of the missing, seemed like cremations.

He had two passions: one for the art of cooking, one for the celebrities who had enjoyed his cooking.

In the art of cooking he was a perfectionist. It would take him days to concoct a sauce. He did his own marketing and waged an unremitting war on all synthetic, frozen, or canned foods.

But in the matter of names he was not so snobbish. He did not question the composition of a famous name. He loved titles, decorations, prizewinners, publicity's favorites.

In Europe he acquired an obsession for quality. In America he acquired gigantism. His dinners grew Gargantuan. His diners had to take walks or dance or swim between dishes.

He took his diners on an Elysian journey of high flavors. His stories poured out like the most suave of his sauces.

As he was as much interested in dishes as in personalities, he gave his dishes the names of people he met. Strawberry Pudding Carole Lombard, Naked Butterfly Irvin S. Cobb, Broiled Oysters George Eastman, Tutti Frutti Edna May Oliver.

Had these personalities flavors which he translated into delicacies? Was Greta Garbo like a flambée, and Julius Bloomfield like borsch? Was William Vanderbilt a crème de France? And Marlene Dietrich a Grenade d'Amour? Was Henry James only capable of evoking shirred eggs, and Sara Delano Roosevelt cinnamon apples, and did Charles Hackett deserve a panache?

But drinks he did not baptize with names of people. They deserved enduring abstractions such as Justice, Liberty, Courage, Democracy.

In the early days of his difficult start in New York he carried home every night some empty bottle of Château d'Yquem which retained its fragrance, and slept on a bench at Long Island station holding the bottle to his nose to make himself dream again of the days when he was serving royalty on the French Riviera. Whereupon he was arrested for alcoholism and vagrancy.

One night he sat in the Paradise Inn kitchen, like a soufflé which had not succeeded. It was late and he was eating some of his own dinner. Renate saw him, and smiled at him through the open partition. He was talking to himself, grumbling.

"Anything troubling you?" asked Renate.

Henri said: "People have lost their palate. All they say is 'More.' It is all those fiery cocktails. They kill the taste. And then they never say the right thing, the kind of thing that puffs me up like a soufflé, the kind of compliment which makes me cook each day better."

"They haven't lost their palate," said Renate, "they have lost their tongue. They haven't lost the power to appreciate your cooking; what they have lost is the power of words. They have never learned culinary language. We live in an Era of Basic English."

"Basic, basic, what is more basic than excellent cooking. You console me, but I still need words, you know, as actors need applause."

"Words have grown scarce. Is that why you so often think of the past? Was it better then?"

"Yes, people had a literary appreciation of cooking. They could describe their sensations and they were eloquent about them. Poor Henri. He does see too many empty chairs. The people who come now are of a different breed. They are sulky and half-mute. They say: 'It is good Henri.' But how good, how does it compare with other recipes, there are so many nuances!"

"It's only language that has grown poor."

"You may be right. Did I ever tell you about Diamond Jim Brady and the twelve oysters? He once ordered me to serve twelve oysters in each of which I was to place a pearl. He was giving a dinner for twelve Ziegfeld girls. He wanted me to do my very best. While I prepared the oysters I noticed I had only eleven pearls, and I got very worried. I called him up and he said: 'Don't worry, Henri. It was done on purpose. The girl who does not get the pearl in the oyster will get a marriage contract from me. You announce it. I can't bring myself to make such a silly announcement as a marriage proposal. I just can't bring myself to say the words.' "

Varda lived on a converted ferry boat in Sausalito and sailed the bay in his own sail boat; so it was surprising to see him arrive at Paradise Inn in an old station wagon bringing his newest collages for an exhibition: "Collages are not sea-faring."

He unloaded them at the entrance and stood them up against the rocky banks in the sunlight. They eclipsed the sun, the sea and the plants. The laminated blues dimmed the refractions of the ocean and made it seem ponderous and opaque. His treble greens vibrated and made the plants seem dead and the flowers artificial. His shafts of gold made the sunrays pale.

With small pieces of cotton and silks, scissors and glue and a dash of paint, he dressed his women in irradiations; his colors breathed like flesh and the fine spun lines pulsated like nerves.

In his landscapes of joy, women became staminated flowers, and flowers women. They were as fragrant as if he had painted them with thyme, saffron and curry. They were translucent and airy, carrying their Arabian Night's cities like nebulous scarves around their lucite necks.

Sometimes they were masked like Venetian beauties at masquerades. They wore necklaces of solar meteorites, and earrings which sang like birds. Velvet petals covered their breasts and stared with enticing eyes. Orange tones played like the notes of a flute. Magenta had a sound of bells. The blues throbbed like the night.

After his scissors had touched them, his women became flowers, plants and sea shells.

He cut into all the legendary textiles of the world: damask of the Medicis, oyster white of Greek robes, the mixed gold and blue of Venetian brocades, the midnight blue wools of Peru, the sand colors of the African cottons, the transparent muslins of India, to give birth to women who only appear to men asleep. His women became comets, trailing long nebulous trains, erratic members of the solar system. He gave only the silver scale of their mermaid moods, the sea shell rose of their ear lobes, corollas, pistils, light as wings. He housed them in façades of tent shelters which could be put up for a moment and folded and vanished when desire expired.

"Nothing endures," said Varda, "unless it has first been transposed into a myth, and the great advantage of myths is that they are ladies with portable roots."

He often spoke of paradise. Paradise was a distillation of women panoplied with ephemeral qualities. His collages taught how to remain in a state of grace of love, extract only elixirs, transmute all life' into lunisolar fiestas, and all women, by a process of cut-outs, to aphrodisiacs.

He was the alchemist searching only for what he could transmute into gold. He never painted homely women, jealous women, or women with colds. He dipped his brushes in pollen, in muteness, in honeymoons, and his women were interchangeable and mobile.

He allowed space and air in their bodies so they would not become too heavy, nor stay too long. He never depicted the death of a love, fatigue or boredom. Every collage was rich with a new harem, the constancy of illusion, fidelity to euphorias born of woman.

He took no time to weep over fadings or witherings; he was always mixing a new brew, a new woman, and when he sat at his large table, scissors in hand, searching for a new marriage of colors, a variation in triangles, in squares and semicircles, interweaving cupolas and breasts, legs and columns, windows and eyes on beds of pleasure, under tent of rituals of the flesh, each color became a music box.

He canonized his women, they bore the names of new brands of sainthood.

Saint Banality, who reigned over the artists who could take everyday objects and turn them into extraordinary ones, like the postman in France who built a castle out of the stones he found on his route every day; the shoe cleaner in Brooklyn who decorated his shoe shine box with medals, unmatched ear-rings, broken glass and silver paper to look like a Byzantine crown; the mason in Los Angeles who built towers out of broken cups, tiles, tea pots and washstands.

There was Saint Perfidia who knew how to destroy the monotony of faithfulness, and Saint Parabola who decorated with haloes those whose stories no one could understand, and Saint Hyperbole who cured of boredom.

Saint Corona arrived at sunrise to wake him, and Saint Erotica visited him at night.

The women were interchangeable and flowed into one another as in dreams. He admitted and loved all of them except women in black. "Black is for widows," he said, for the severe women who had raised him in Greece, for women in churches and women in cemeteries. Black was the absence of color.

He saw women as feathers, furs, meteorites, lace, campaniles, filigree; and so he was more amazed than other fathers to find his own daughter made of other substances like a colorless doll lying inside a magician's trunk, with eyes not quite blue, hair not quite gold, as if she had been the only one he had forgotten to paint.

When she was six years old he felt there was yet time, that it was merely because he had never painted children, and that his gift for painting women would become effective on the day of her womanhood. At seven years of age she listened to his stories and believed them, and he felt that with patience, luminosity and plumage would grow.

A tall, very strong woman came to visit Varda, and the gossips whispered that she was a gangster's moll. When she saw Varda's daughter she said: "Varda, would you mind if someday I kidnapped your daughter?"

This frightened her and every evening before going to bed she would ask: "She won't come and kidnap me while I'm asleep, will she?"

"No," said Varda, "she can't take you away without my permission, and I won't let her. She has tried to bribe me. She came this morning in a boat loaded with sacks of sugar and sacks of fruit (and you know how much I love them) to exchange for you and I said, 'No, I love my daughter and you can take back your sugar and your fruit.'"

The next evening at bedtime Varda said: "Today the kidnapper came with a hundred bottles of red wine (and you know how much I love wine) and I told her that I loved my daughter and didn't want any wine."

And the next evening he told her: "She was here with a hundred elephants (and you know how much I love elephants) and I sent her away."

Each day she awaited new proofs of her father's love. One day he turned down a hundred camels left over from a film, and then a hundred sacks of paint (and she knew how much Varda loved paint) and then a hundred sacks of bits of cloth for his collages, beautiful fragments from all over the world (and she knew how much he loved textiles).

And then Varda said one evening: "The kidnapper thought of the most diabolical offer of all. What do you think it was? She had a hundred little girls, just like you, with blue eyes and blond hair and willowy figures, and all fit for a harem and once again (though I was sorely tempted) I said, 'No, I love my own girl best of all.'"

But in spite of the stories, it was as if she had determined to grow contrary to all the women he loved. She let her hair fall as it willed, never brushing it to bring out the gloss. She wore faded jeans and greasy tennis sneakers. She shredded the edge of her jeans so they would look like those of beggars on the stage. She wore Varda's torn shirts and discarded sweaters and went out with boys more sullen and mute than herself.

On her fifteenth birthday when he expected a metamorphosis as spectacular as that of a butterfly, she wrote him a long reproachful letter from school asking him to give up "those women." She said that she would not stay with him anymore while those flashy, glittering women were about.

She doubted his prestidigitations with words, as if he were

a stage magician, as if to say: "See, they have no effect on me. I do not believe in fairy tales. I am going to study science."

When she came on holiday Varda told her another story: "There was a woman from Albania who was famous for her beauty. A young man from America came, very handsome, slim and blond and he paid court to her and said: 'I love you because you remind me of a cousin of mine I loved when I was in school. You also remind me of a movie actress I always adored on the screen. I love you. Will you marry me?' The Albanian girl took a small pistol out of her boot and shot him. When she was brought to trial the old Albanian judge listened with sympathy as she made her own defense. 'Your honor, I have been humiliated several times in my life.' 'How could that be,' said the judge, 'you are such a beautiful woman.' 'Yes, your honor, it has happened. I was humiliated the first time by a man who left me waiting in church when we were to be married. He was in a car accident, it is true, but still in my family there is a tradition of unfailing courtesy about marriage ceremonies. The second time I was told by a Frenchman that I was too fat. The third time I was "clocked" by a policeman on a motorcycle. He said I had been speeding and I contradicted him and he said he had "clocked" me. Imagine that. But, your honor, I never killed before. You know Albanian pride. Until this American came and told me I reminded him of two other women, and that, your honor, was too much. He offended my uniqueness.'"

She shrugged her shoulders. "Women in Albania do not carry pistols in their boots. And who wants to be unique anyway? It's a dated concept."

When she criticized modern painting he tried to explain the state of painting today.

"There was a painter who was asked to send his best painting to an exhibition and he accepted on condition that it would be curtained off until the day of the opening. This condition was accepted. The crowd came, quite a large one. His painting was the only one hidden behind a curtain in a box, and the last to be exposed. When the curtain was finally parted, the painting was a large square canvas, pure blank. Blank! The public was outraged. There were insults: 'Surrealist! Dadaist! Beatnik! Mutant!' Then the painter came forward and explained that he had painted a self-portrait and that his dog had found it such an exact likeness that he had licked it all off. But there had been a portrait, and this was merely the proof of the faithfulness of the likeness. And so, dear daughter, for those who are interested in progress, twenty years ago painting was judged by critics, and today it is judged by a dog. This is the state of painting today."

Varda also had a theory on uncouth manners which he told very often in the presence of his daughter's sulky visitors.

"This is a modernized version of the Princess and the Dragon. Today she would be the Imperial Valley Lettuce Queen and the young man could be any one of you. The dragon had to be killed before the young man could marry the girl. The dragon had a corrugated skin, bluish and silvery and scaly like a mirror broken into a thousand small pieces. His eyes wept chronically. He spouted fire with the regularity of a lighter. The young man turned off the gas first and then cut off the dragon's head. He took the beauty queen brusquely by the arm and pushing her ahead of him said in a Humphrey Bogart style of speech: 'Oh, come on, we've wasted enough time on the old dragon. I've got a motel room waiting.' The queen looked at the expiring dragon weeping at her leaving, and suddenly she put her arms around the beast and said: 'I'll stay with him. I don't like the rough tone of your voice.' And as she encircled the scaly dragon, he turned into a young man handsomer and tenderer than the one she had jilted."

His daughter shrugged her shoulders, blew into her bubble gum of a pink Varda had never in all his life conceded to use, counted her new freckles, and went back to her science homework.

She was chewing the end of her pencil while she studied a chemical which produced visions and hallucinations. She read to her father in a flat-toned voice the effect of consciousness-expanding chemicals.

"Colors breathe and emit light."

"But my colors do that," said Varda.

"Figures dissolve into one another and appear at times transparent."

"As they do in my collages," said Varda.

"Someone saw whirling clouds, suns and moons," she read in the same voice as she might have read: "Imperial Valley produced 20,000 head of lettuce."

"As in the paintings of Van Gogh," said Varda. "What need of chemicals?"

"But when you take a chemical you know it will affect you for only a few hours and then you will return to normality. You can control it, modify it, you can even stop its effects if you wish to, if you don't like what is happening to you."

"In other words, a return ticket," said Varda.

"The next day the world is back again in its proper place, the real colors are back."

"Doesn't that prove that when you remove an inhibiting consciousness and let men dream they all dream like painters or poets?"

"But you dream all the time, whereas a pill is more scientific."

Perhaps science would illumine his cautious child. Perhaps by way of a chemical she might respond, vibrate, shine? He watched the eyelashes pulled down like shades, the ears covered by hair, the lips parsimonious of words.

What had he absorbed through the years which had opened these worlds to him which others sought in mushrooms? Where had he learned the secret of phosphorescence, of illumination, of transfiguration? Where had he learned to take the shabbiest materials and heighten them with paint, alter their shapes with scissors?

"What I wanted to teach you is contained in one page of the dictionary. It is all the words beginning with *trans*: transfigure, transport, transcend, translucent, transgression, transform, transmit, transmute, transpire, all the trans-Siberian voyages."

"You forgot the word transvestite."

"When I was ten years old I made up my first story."

"I'm going to be late for my expanding-consciousness lecture!"

"This is a very short story. It's about a blind old man who had a daughter. This daughter described to him every day the world they lived in, the people who came to see him, the beauty of their house, garden, friends. One day a new doctor came to town and he cured the old man's blindness. When he was able to see, he discovered they had been living in a shack, on an empty lot full of debris, that their friends had been hoboes and drunks. His daughter was crying, thinking he would die of shock, but his reaction was quite the opposite. He said to her: 'It is true that the world you described does not exist but as you built that image so carefully in my mind and I can still see it so vividly, we can now set about to build it just as you made me see it.'"

His daughter remained neutral, and as silent as her rubber-soled tennis shoes. She hung her long legs over the edge of the deck and swung them like a boy. She dissected snails.

"Such cruelty," said Varda.

"Not at all," she said with a newborn scientist's arrogance. "They have no nervous system."

Meanwhile Varda continued to make collages as some women light votive candles. With scissors and glue and small pieces of fabrics, he continued to invent women who glittered, charmed, levitated and wore luminous aureoles like saints. But his daughter resisted all her father's potions, as if she had decided from the day she was born never to become one of the women he cut out in the shape of circles, triangles, cubes, to suit the changing forms of his desires.

And then one day after she had been away for a few days she wrote Varda the following letter:

"Before I took the chemical called L.S.D., it was as if light, color, smell and touch could not reach me. It was as if I were

66

outside looking through glass. But that day (I think it was the second time) I was finally *inside*. I looked at the rug on the floor and it was no longer a plain rug but a moving and swaying mass like hair floating on water or like wind over a field of wheat. The door knob ceased to be a plain door knob. It melted and undulated and the door opened and all the walls and windows vanished. There was a tremor of life in everything. The once static objects in the room all flowed into a fluid and mobile and breathing world. The dazzle of the sun was multiplied, every speck of gold and diamond in it magnified. Trees, skies, clouds, lawns began to breathe, heave and waver like a landscape at the bottom of the sea. My body was both swimming and flying. I felt gay and at ease and playful. There was perfect communicability between my body and everything surrounding me. The singing of the mocking-birds was multiplied, became a whole forest of singing birds. My senses were multiplied as if I had a hundred eyes, a hundred ears, a hundred fingertips. On the walls appeared endless murals of designs I made which produced their own music to match. When I drew a long orange line it emitted its own orange tone. The music vibrated through my body as if I were one of the instruments and I felt myself becoming a full percussion orchestra, becoming green, blue, orange, gold. The waves of the sounds ran through my hair like a caress. The music ran down my back and came out my fingertips. I was a cascade of red blue rainfall, a rainbow. I was small, light, mobile. I could use any method of levitation I wished. I could dissolve, melt, float, soar. Wavelets of light touched the rim of my clothes, phosphorescent radiations. I could see a new world with my middle eye, a world I had missed before. I caught images behind images, the walls behind the sky, the sky behind the Infinite. The walls became fountains, the fountains became arches, the arches domes, the domes sky, the sky a flowering carpet, and all dissolved into pure space. I looked at a slender line curving over space which disappeared into infinity. I saw a million zeroes on this line, curving, shrinking in the distance and I laughed and said 'Excuse me, I am not a mathematician.' How can I measure the infinite? But I understand it. The zeroes vanished. I was standing on the rim of a planet, alone. I could hear the fast rushing sounds of the planets rotating in space. Then I was among them, and I was aware that a certain skill was necessary to handle this new means of transportation. The image of myself standing in space and trying to get my 'sea legs' or my 'space legs' amused me. I *wondered who had been there before me* and whether I could return to earth. The solitude distressed me, so I returned to my starting point. I was standing in front of an ugly garden door. But as I looked closer it was not plain or green but it was a Buddhist temple, a Hindu colonnade, Moroccan mosaic ceiling, gold spires being formed and re-formed as if I were watching the hand of a designer at work. I was designing spirals of red unfurled until they formed a rose window or a *mandala* with edges of radium. When one design was barely born and arranged itself, it dissolved and the next one followed without confusion. Each form, each line emitted its equivalent in music in perfect accord with the design. An undulating line emitted a sustained undulating melody, a circle had a corresponding musical notation, diaphanous colors, diaphanous sounds, a pyramid created a pyramid of ascending notes, and vanishing ones left only an echo. These designs were preparatory sketches for entire Oriental cities. I saw the temples of Java, Kashmir, Nepal, Ceylon, Burma, Cambodia, in all the colors of precious stones illumined from within. Then the outer forms of the temples dissolved to reveal the inner chapel and shrines. The reds and the gold inside the temples created an intricate musical orchestration like Balinese music. Two sensations began to torment me: one that it was happening too quickly and that I would not be able to remember it, another *that I would not be able to tell what I saw,* it was too elusive and too overwhelming. The temples grew taller, the music wilder, it became a tidal wave of sounds with gongs and bells predominating. Gold spires emitted a long flute chant. Every line and color was breathing and constantly mutating. The smoke of my cigarette became gold. The curtain on the window became gold. Then I felt my whole body becoming gold, liquid gold, scintillating warm gold. I WAS GOLD. It was the most pleasurable sensation I have ever known and I knew it was like passion. It was the secret of life, the alchemist's secret of life.

"When I gradually returned from this dream-like experience I was in your studio. I looked around at your collages and recognized them. It was as if I had been there for the first time. I saw the colors, the luminosity and the floating, mobile, changeable quality. I understood all your stories, and all you had said to me. I could see why you had made your women transparent, and the houses open like lace so that space and freedom could blow through them."

When she came home on vacation, she had emerged from her grey cocoon. She was now sixteen and sending forth her first radiations and vibrations dressed in Varda's own rutilant colors.

WHEN RENATE AND VARDA MET AT PARADISE INN SHE HAD BEEN touched by the story of his daughter. Secretly she wished she had had a father who was a magician with colors and who would have told her stories. To please him she wore a cotton dress in colors which recalled the dresses of his women. Her coat was lined with pale stripes of violet, white and green which immediately attracted Varda's attention. He was as excited by a new combination of tones or materials as other men might be by a new dish, or a new brand of paint. He was always searching for pieces of textiles for his collages. He caressed the lining of Renate's coat with delight.

To his amazement Renate took a big pair of scissors from the kitchen and before his eyes she cut out a piece big enough to dress one of his abstract women.

Varda spent a few days at the inn. There were many parties given for him. At these parties the two painters dazzled each other like two magicians practicing all their spells and charms upon each other.

But the friendship remained aerial, like two acrobats speaking to each other only when hundreds of feet above the crowd.

Speaking of modern painting Renate said: "So many of them lack taste."

"What they lack is distaste," said Varda.

They laughed together, but the distance remained.

One day Varda absorbed some of Henri's best wine, the one which fermented the highest content of eloquence, and he confessed to him: "Renate is marvelous."

"She is marvelous," echoed Henri. "I'm going to name a dessert after her."

"She is *femme toute faite*."

"*Toute faite?*"

"Already designed, completed, perfect in every detail."

"You say this as if it were not a compliment."

70

"I only say it regretfully, Henri. For I myself, I need un-formed women, unfinished, undesigned women I can mold to my own pattern. I'm an artist. I'm only looking for fragments, remnants which I can co-ordinate in a new way. A woman ar-tist makes her own patterns."

"A good recipe for other women," said Henri.

Bruce and Renate entered a dimly-lit cafe where anyone could sit on the small stage and sing folk songs, and if he sang well would be kept there by applause and, if not, quickly encouraged to leave. The tables were beer-stained and sticky with Coca-Cola. The waitresses were heavily made up with Cleopatra eyes, and they wore sack dresses and black stockings. The spotlight on the singers was red and made them appear pale and condemned to sing. The shadows were so strong that when they bent over their guitar it seemed suggestively intimate and not like a song one must listen to. A few figures stood in the shadows on the side, and from this vague group a woman sprang towards them and, touching Renate's arm, said in a chanting voice: "You are Renate," giving to the name all the musical resonances it contained and adding, with a perfect lyrical illogic: "I am Nina," as if a woman called Nina must of course address a woman called Renate. Renate hesitated because she was trying to remember where she had seen Nina and yet she could not remember, and this was so manifest on her face that Nina said: "Of course you could not remember, there are fourteen women in me, you may have met only one of them, perhaps on the stage, when I acted at the Playwright's Theatre, do you remember that? I was the blind girl."

"Yes, of course I remember her, but you do not seem like the same woman, and even now you do not seem like the same woman who first came out to speak to me."

It was true that she changed so quickly that already Renate had seen in her a beautiful Medea because of the flowing hair, but a Medea without jealousy, and the next moment she seemed like a wandering Ophelia who had never known repose. It was impossible to imagine her asleep or drowned. She held her head proudly on a very slender neck; she used her hands like puppets, each finger with an important role to play. She was without sadness and so light she seemed almost weightless, as if performing on a stage alone, while her eyes scanned the entire room, her quick-winged words a monologue about to be interrupted. She thrust out her shoulders as if she had to push her way through a crowd and leave.

Bruce's speech and thoughts were agile, like those of a rootless person accustomed to pack and move swiftly from city to city, from home to home, and yet he could not follow her flights and vertiginous transitions. A touching, apologetic smile accompanied her incoherence. She herself did not get lost in sudden turns and free associations, but she seemed wistful that others could not follow her.

"My name is Nina Gitana de la Primavera." She said "Gitana" as if she had been born in Spain, and "Primavera" as if she had been born in Italy, and one could see the Persian flowers on her cotton dress flowering.

"But these are my winter names. I change with the seasons. When the spring comes I no longer need to be Primavera. I leave that to the season. It is so far away." She threw her head back like a young horse trying to sniff the far off spring, so far back Renate thought her neck would snap.

"I am waiting for Manfred, but he is not coming. May I sit with you?"

"Who is Manfred?" asked Bruce.

She repeated the name but separated its syllables: "Man-fred." As if she were examining its philological roots.

"Man-fred is the man I am going to love. He may not yet be born. I have often loved men who are not yet born."

Bruce, who never swerved in the path of a drunkard, who had once invited a potential burglar to come in for a coffee, was afraid of this beautiful undrowned Ophelia who borrowed her language from mythology. He feared she had the power to snap the cord which bound him securely to ordinary life.

He wanted to leave. But just then a new singer climbed the wooden stage, and began to talk before he sang as if to sell his own songs.

Nina never ceased talking except to stare at Renate and Bruce and touch their faces delicately with her fingertips as if she were still playing the blind girl on the stage. Then she spread open her hands and to each separate finger she said severely: "You talk too much."

Renate wondered how anyone had been able to put the words of playwrights in her mouth when her own overflowed so profusely. But she was able to quote Gertrude Stein accurately and sing a Mozart theme when she mentioned the composer. So her memory was not lost in this multitude of disconnected selves.

Bruce asked her questions as if he were a reporter interviewing her, but a reporter accustomed to deal with the poetics of space, air and water.

"Say something I will always remember," he asked, thinking that in this way he might solve the elusive nature of her talk.

She meditated silently and then gracefully made five gestures. She touched her forehead, her lips, her breasts, the center of her throat, then placed her hand under her elbow and held it there and said: "Remember this."

"As-tar-te,'" she murmured. "Every word has several personalities enclosed in it, and if you separate the syllables you can catch all its aspects. Bruce is too short for you. It does not describe you. Have you ever noticed how short American names are? They are like lizards who have lost their tails. This happened when America was first settled. It was a rebellion against the long European names. You should have a name like a merry-go-round. It should have a joyous sound, and it should *turn*."

Her body was thin and supple. Her eyes large and green. She had a pure straight nose, finely designed lean cheeks, a tender but not too full mouth and beautiful teeth. Her long curled hair covered her shoulders. On stage she looked like Vivien Leigh. In life she looked as if she had dressed in old stage clothes, an Indian print cotton not made for her, which was off the shoulders and which she was too thin to hold up securely, covered by a dusty violet cape.

Every now and then she exposed her teeth, placed a finger on the middle tooth and hissed as if she wanted to let the breath out of her body, like a balloon about to fly. With a long thin finger she designed a large S on the bar table, explaining that this was the sign of the Infinite. The hiss had been a prologue to S S S S S S.

"Julien and his wife do not want me to go out alone because they think I am mad and that the madhouse people will pick me up and that they will give a shock treatment to wake me up."

"You are dreaming awake," said Renate. "Many people dream awake. And some are jealous of having no dreams and they either drink or take pills to make them dream."

"I am not going home to Julien and Juliana tonight. I love them but that is not my home tonight. I must find my real home tonight. The police will not let me sit on trees. I did once at Pershing Square. I loved climbing the tree there, and listening to the preachers, and watching the hoboes who listen to the songs and the prayers. They were all lost people like me, and even their clothes did not belong to them. You could see they were dressed with what people gave to charity collections and from Thrift Shops. Each piece of clothing had belonged to a different human being. I sat up there for a whole evening but then I could not get down again. And when the police found me they took me to a big building and they gave me a shock to wake me up. Silver Fox said to me once, 'Nina, you have something to give to the world and the world has nothing to give you.'"

"Who is Silver Fox?" asked Bruce who was determined to find a key and had hopes that this story would make sense and that he might identify the characters.

Each word came out of her mouth caressed as if it were a beautiful word, a sensuous word. When Bruce asked his questions she looked as if her magic trick had failed. But she was indulgent towards his blindness.

She drank wine, and when the glass was empty she held it against her cheek as if to warm it, and no one could have sworn they had seen her drink. Towards midnight she refused another glass but said she was hungry. She paused to try and remember when she had last eaten. "Oh, yes, last night."

So Bruce ordered a sandwich. It was a big Italian sandwich, clumsy and as large as her face. Before starting she pulled up her dress once more because her breasts were too small to hold its strapless top. Then she handled the sandwich as if it were a wafer. She looked mischievously at Bruce as if she knew he did not believe she would eat it, and he was amazed to see it vanish while her eyes remaining fixed on him seemed to say: "I will swallow it but you won't see me eat it."

"You have magical powers," said Renate, "and yet Bruce and I feel we must protect you. Bruce and I will take you wherever you want to go tonight."

Nina asked for the time, although Renate was sure she did not care. It was part of her exquisite politeness towards conventions. Nina braided her long hair and took her bracelet off in preparation for the journey.

"People are afraid of dreamers," she said. "They want to put me away."

On the pavement they found giant pipelines resting beside an excavated street. Nina bent over one of the openings and laughed into the drainpipe and then ran towards the other end to see if her laughter was coming out of it.

The friend she wanted to stay with was not in. So Renate and Bruce drove her to Malibu. She thought the room was small; then she opened the window and said: "Oh, but there is so much more to this room than I thought. It's enormous. There is a roar in my ears."

"It's the ocean," said Renate.

Then Nina asked for silver foil paper. "I always glue silver foil paper on the walls to make them beautiful."

She wanted to mop the tile floor with beer. "The foam will make it shine."

"Do you want to sleep?" asked Renate.

"I never sleep," said Nina. "Just give me a sheet."

She took the sheet and covered herself with it, and then slid to the floor saying: "Now I am invisible."

The next day she wanted to go to the theatre. There was a play she had already seen but wanted to see again.

She carried a brown paper bag with her which she would not allow Bruce to leave in the car when they entered the theatre.

During the play there was a scene at a dining-table. The actors sat around talking and eating. At this point Nina opened her brown paper bag, took out a sandwich and a pickle and began to eat in unison with the actors. She whispered to Renate: "The audience should not just watch actors eat. They should eat with them. They will feel less lonely."

Then she laughed softly: "I have a friend who says the best way to remember a beautiful city or a beautiful painting is to eat something while you are looking at it. The flavor really helps the image to penetrate the body. It fixes it as lacquer does a drawing."

After the performance she insisted on visiting the actors. "I don't know any of them but they like to see friendly faces."

A friend hailed her. He was a television actor. He took her arm and guided her out of the theatre.

Bruce and Renate did not see her for several days. Then she reappeared one day and she was wearing a new dress and new sandals.

"I got a job," she said. "Do you remember the young actor we met at the theatre? They had just finished a reading of a children's play for a radio show but the star could not laugh like a witch. He remembered that I had done this once to frighten people at a party I did not like. So they put me in this sound-proof room. I could see the men behind the glass windows running their machines. They wore earphones and never raised their eyes to see what I was doing. They blinked some red lights and I heard a voice say: 'Now start laughing like a witch until I tell you to stop.' I felt that I must laugh, must keep on laughing and attract their attention, or else they would leave me in that room and forget all about me. I was all alone in a room without echoes. You don't know the loneliness of being in a room without echo. I had to laugh like a witch with nobody to laugh for, or to laugh at. To wind myself up I went to each corner of the room pretending each corner was a different person, and I laughed, laughed, and finally I was laughing so hard I was afraid I could not stop. I thought if no one comes into the room, if no human being comes in and says: 'It is enough,' I will not be able to stop. I watched the wheels turning and hoped the tape would give out. And finally it did give out and its tail rose up like the tail of a snake and it slapped the young man in the face, the young man who would not look at me. Then the young man opened the door and said to me: 'We got a lot of footage out of that,' and handed me a check. I bought this dress, do you like it? See, it is wide and loose like a tent. All I need to do is pull it up a little above my head, and then sink down, and I am completely covered and can go to sleep. And do you like my sandals? I brought you a present. I found her waiting for an audition."

It was Nobuko who came walking over the small stones of the patio with short, tiny steps. Though she had walked up the hill from the bus stop, no dust showed on her white socks and wooden sandals. She was carrying flowers she had picked up on the way, which she offered to Renate.

NOBUKO WAS SMALL AND DAINTY. SHE CARRIED HER HEAD HEAVY
with the bun of glossy black hair on a delicate neck gently undulating as in classical Japanese prints. The flawless golden skin at
the nape of the neck exposed by the open collar of the kimono
attracted the eye with a delicate yielding quality and had been
justly declared an erotic zone. She had a chanting child-like
voice, a laugh like windchimes and a graceful way of standing
and sitting creating an aesthetic delight. Her eyes were small,
narrow, intensely brilliant; her nose had almost no bone like the
nose of a child. She kept a precarious balance between sprite,
woman and child. Her face was the face of the moon become
woman. Her talk was light and breathless, with a tone of voice
ranging from song to dove's cooing to a schoolgirl's laughter in
forbidden places.

She wore a kimono of white cotton embroidered with eyelets,
and over this a black transparent one, the layer of white like the
pearly glaze of pottery, a bride seen through a widow's veil. The
obi was red. On the back of her black silk coat appeared a large
red chrysanthemum.

"I must apologize, because in Japan my mother owns a kimono for each day of the year as each design must match the
season and the flower or plant in bloom that day. I should not
be wearing chrysanthemums in February when they only bloom
in May. I would like to learn American freedom in clothes, in
everything. I would like to be like you, Renate, you are the
freest woman I know. I only saw such freedom in Italy where
they are so natural, and in Japan everything is unnatural."

With her two index fingers she held up the corners of her
mouth into an exaggerated grin. "We must always smile," and
then dropped her lids and mimicked a flood of tears falling from
her eyes, "even when we feel like weeping."

They were all sitting at the beach, and Renate offered her a
drink in a paper cup.

79

"It is not a very beautiful cup," said Renate.

"But it seems beautiful to me because it is so simple, it does not require a ceremony, to be polished, and served on the right tray at the right moment. Everything is so simple here. In my country I was considered a very advanced girl. But ever since I have started to travel in order to become an actress I have learned that I am still bound to tradition and conventions. When I went to Paris I was invited for a week-end in the country. The young people had a guest house of their own. It was called *La Maison des Oiseaux*. (When Nobuko said *"oiscaux"* it sounded like the sibilance of bees, of breeze.) I was so formal and proper. They were sweet about my fears. I came to America to learn to be free. Ancient beliefs are still so strong in Japan, tradition is imposed on us by our parents, but the new Japan pulls us away, the young are caught in this conflict. We cannot emancipate ourselves if we stay there, we must get away. I love my family and I do not like to offend them. I do not feel free."

Renate had just visited cherry blossom trees grown by Japanese gardeners. Nobuko laughed at Renate's admiration of the cherry blossoms. "They are so silly, they bloom so briefly, and the rest of the time they drop worms on our hairdos."

When Nobuko spoke of intimate things like the *Maison des Oiseaux*, she bowed her head and closed her eyes as if she were in a confessional. She locked her small hands as if to pray for this new Nobuko trying to be born.

Nobuko was given the role of Cassandra in *Trojan Women* of Euripides. She struggled to emerge from her Japanese print movements. She rolled over rocks, fell on her knees, shook her long black hair and collapsed in disordered grief. It was a caricature of a Western interpretation of Greek tragedy. One feared to see her snap her fragile neck, or force the exquisite lines out of shape forever.

After the play, receiving visitors and compliments, she held her small hand before her mouth as if to screen the new bold words she might utter, as if to muffle their effect.

All through rehearsals she avoided using the word "rape."

She talked about the Sabine women being deflowered. "The characterization of Cassandra," she said, "'is still a conflict between the director and the chorus." But for Nobuko it seemed more like a conflict between a Western interpretation of Greek tragedy as chaos and a classical Japanese elegance of style.

"Renate, please don't bother yourself to go beyond what you can do for my acting career, only what comes neatly in your way."

The second visit she made Renate, she wore a yellow silk kimono and carried a small basket. With her black hair high on her head, she looked like a giant sunflower with a black velvet core swaying in the fields.

She opened the smallest pill box in the world to take out a sucaril tablet.

"I was given a film test today. It was for a Western, and they shoot so promiscuously."

Another time she wore a dove grey kimono with an orange obi, and she let her head incline to one side as the tulips do at night.

"Renate, I'm at a loss what to do with my tremendously long and unknown future. I'm really not so sure I'll be able to accomplish what I've dreamed of, what I'm searching for."

It was now the month of May. Nobuko wore a kimono embroidered with a purple jacaranda bloom, with a gold obi. At last she felt in harmony with nature's designs.

"All I want, Renate, is not to be a good-for-nothing."

Renate painted a portrait of her. While Renate worked Nobuko watched her freedom of movements, freedom of dress, her quick responses and inventive language.

And then it was time to leave.

From New York she wrote on purple tissue paper because the sun was absent. She sent Renate photographs. "Two are loud and embarrassing for commercials, but the small one is in a funny way old-fashioned and natural, so this is for my dear person Renate. I have understood very well what you have explained about independence. It is obvious that life and career in Japan must be much easier and less strenuous, but I consider myself so fortunate to be able to taste the bitter sweet of freedom. Vaulting ambition in theatrical experiment and the obsession not to be a good-for-nothing in addition to impatience and restlessness cause me a lot of worry."

Another letter came in orange tissue paper because the sun was out: "My plant, just a simple rubber plant, is growing energetically, and it does tell me spring is here. I know this is the end of my very dear and most thrilling season of life. I mean to leave America and plunge into the Japanese theatre world, and this is a very strangely complex feeling. Youth, Passion, Dreams and a long long future . . . They are quite frightening to me. Such a great responsibility. If I were to end up as a good-for-nothing. Renate, the other night I was awe-stricken, truthfully, when I realized that if you love someone else dearly, for example my parents, my sister . . . You can't even have the last freedom that you possess, the free choice of death . . ."

Renate could see Nobuko bound in her enveloping kimono, the wide sleeves like closed wings against her body, the feet in white cotton and sandals, seeking to shake off the ritualistic past, the thoughtful meditative forms, the contained stylizations, and she wondered whether she could emerge from centuries of confinement.

Nobuko wrote: "I could not write you yesterday because it was raining and I did not find any pearl grey paper to match."

THE FRENCH CONSULATE WAS HOUSED IN A PSEUDO-SPANISH HOUSE at the top of the Hollywood Hills. It conformed in no way to the Hollywood expectations about a French Consulate. The French Consul was a novelist, his wife wrote biographies, the secretary who opened the door did not look like Brigitte Bardot, the desk at the entrance was plain, the rooms were not furnished in Louis XVI style, nor in the fourteenth-century style, nor Empire.

The bar was concealed by New Orleans shutters. There were old Turkish rugs on the tile floor. The pillows around the fireplace were from Thailand. There were French modern paintings on the walls and a Russian icon. The black lacquer furniture was pseudo-Chinese.

The secretary was not coquettish. She was dressed in a plain black sheath and wore two yards of dime store pearls. She led Renate to the living-room. On the way to the living-room Renate noticed the table covered with magazines. They were not risqué. They were art magazines, one of them on the new churches built in France with abstract Christs and abstract Madonnas painted by modern painters.

The Consul stood near the door. He was slight of build, with large sea-green eyes, a southern skin, and a mouth whose design was marred by a contraction of the upper lip which gave him an air of sneering, or of pouting, a twist which gave his whole face an ambiguous expression. He might have been a conventionally handsome man, but this sneer gave him a slightly sinister air. Renate was to learn later in the evening that it was due to a wound he had received during the war, and then she was distressed to think she had judged his character from his facial design and that this design had been distorted by external circumstances. She tried to reconstruct his face as it might have been before the war. She wondered if this wound had influenced his moods too, for she had heard that he was melancholic in private and gay and witty in public. At the door he had kissed her hand and said to her: "We are celebrating a literary prize I received for my book." He said this in a wistful tone. Renate asked with her natural frankness: "You do not seem to be rejoicing over it."

"It's true, but that's because it came too late."

"Too late! But you're at the prime of life!"

"It came too late, just the same, too late for my mother to know about it. She died during the war. It was she who wanted me to become a famous writer. I did it for her. Now it does not seem to matter very much. Why do I write? What does it bring me? One either fails in one's art or in one's life."

"Look what your writing brings you. You are surrounded by beautiful women, your books are being filmed, you travel, and everywhere you go you have friends. I wanted to meet Jean Delatouche. I was attracted to his imagination and his wit."

"And you'll be disappointed when I tell you I am not Jean."

"You mean, you are no longer Jean. You have become some-one else."

"I never was Jean. I was the non-hero of the book, the half-gangster, the ambiguous adventurer. The hero was the man my mother wanted me to be. The gangster was me. The man you came to see is the hero of the book. The world I create I leave behind me, like an old skin."

The Consul's wife was English. She extended a pale blonde hand, her delicately tinted face and pale blonde hair were almost eclipsed by a Chinese mandarin coat, heavily embroidered. When Renate admired it she said: "It conceals the bulges." Then looking wistfully at the Consul who did not kiss all the women's hands, only the pretty ones, she added: "Other people have breakdowns when they do not succeed. He has them when he has a success which his mother cannot enjoy. He is only really happy when he is locked upstairs with his writing."

The Consul was opening the champagne delivered by the French Navy. He wore both martial and literary decorations. He made everyone laugh with sallies and remarks he made with-out smiling. Most of the time he did not appear at parties, but let his wife officiate. Visitors sometimes caught sight of him as he opened his window for a little fresh air and then his wife would say: "He is working on his novel."

The patio evoked Algerian settings. It was sheltered by a pepper tree and the Consul's wife had decorated it with Moroccan rugs and a Turkish coffee set of copper inlaid with floral designs.

The cook was Russian. Her hobby was collecting stray cats and injured dogs. More often when she came to the salon it was not to bring ice but to ask the Consul's wife for bandages or aspirin for the animals. The ice never came, but the Consul's wife told the Westerners in love with space about the advice given to her by her Russian maid which had proved valuable: "When your thoughts have too much space, they fly off into the infinite. It is necessary to work and think in an enclosed room, then the thoughts cannot escape. They rebound."

Officially, publicly, in the eyes of the world, publishers, magazines, and television people, it was he who was the writer. His books were known, he had received prizes, and films were being made of them. Very few people knew that the Consul's wife was a writer too.

She had written a vivid book about four English women who had wanted to escape from England to the Orient, had wanted an adventurous life, and had all succeeded and fulfilled their desires richly and fully.

She was herself physically such an exact replica of the delicately tinted women of English paintings that it was difficult to remember her features. The shell rose, the faintly drawn features were always about to vanish in one's memory. Her smile, her pale blue glance were all evanescent. One could not at first relate her to the characters she had painted in such rich colors, women of daring, of defiance towards conventions, and above all, women who had been led completely by their passions and their whims.

They seemed so distinct from her that Renate wondered how

she had selected them and lived in intimacy with them during years of library research in many cities.

But the link between them appeared gradually and subtly. She had lived in the consulates of the countries she described. The antique Turkish rug on the floor did not come from a Turkish bazaar. In Los Angeles she had discovered a Turkish rug merchant in a plain and homely street. Her knowledge of the language was so perfect that the merchant had invited her to have native coffee with him. In an enormous loft all the rugs were piled up upon one another. And it was on top of them, at least two yards from the floor, that he had the copper tray put down for them to squat by, Turkish fashion.

She had already too many rugs and her husband complained but she could not resist taking another one home now and then.

The last one was so ancient that only the backing showed, and very little of the colored wool's design, but she knew what this design had been.

She even preferred to re-weave these missing fragments in her mind. It was a spiritual discipline which enabled her, sitting in the California patio, to re-weave the fragments of her life in foreign places. She could find the smell and colors of those evenings spent sitting on the cream white roofs of Turkish houses, not on chairs but on Turkish rugs and pillows. She could see every flower, leaf, tendril reborn as a lyric melody of warm colors like the colors of her life with the Consul. She could re-live visits to the bazaars and cafés, night in the desert in Arab costumes, scenes of dances, of tribal war rehearsals, and hear the melodies, chantings and laments while smoking opium.

Many times it was she who explored the labyrinthian cities of the Orient while the Consul stayed in his room to write. So that when she came to write the biographies of those adventurous exiled English women, she knew the clothes they wore, the food they ate, the contents of their trunks, baskets, and handbags, details about the furniture, the insides of the houses, contents of caravans, the talk of servants. Her husband said "She was always buying things in bazaars, things we did not need, which we had to carry about." He did not know she was collecting props which later she used lovingly in her biographies.

In Los Angeles her bed had a muslin canopy such as she must have had as a young girl, and Renate felt that within the mature woman a young and virginal adolescent was still sleeping under her first communion and wedding dress innocence. It was the bed of an unawakened woman, and even though grey hairs showed at the roots of the grey-blonde hair, the pale blue ribbon which bound it proclaimed a freakish error in nature's calculations. It had a buoyant air, an undaunted flying pennant which may explain why only surprise showed in her eyes when the Consul confessed his obsession with young girls.

The walls were covered with photographs of the four women she had written about, who resembled her so much that her face could have been substituted for all of them.

Bruce had to appear in a television show so he left the party early, and much later Renate was placed in a taxi by the Consul, with a taxi driver he knew so that he felt she would be safely driven home.

The taxi driver wore a beret and rather long hair. "I'm a painter from Marseilles. The Consul and I made friends during the war. I drive him about. I'm his private chauffeur for special errands. We are drinking pals. I know him probably better than anyone, because we are bottle brothers. We both love wine and we both love women. I know his mistress. She's a girl from Algiers. I sometimes drive her to the Consulate when he is alone. In fact, I know him better than you can ever imagine. Because I know him when he needs to escape from that role he plays, of diplomat, public figure, gentleman of letters, friend of prominent men. I know him when he wishes to drown the world he lives in because it doesn't mean anything to him, and find girls he can talk roughly to, and does not need to be witty, or gallant, or kiss hands, or open car doors. With me he drinks all night; he knows I will drive him back safely and the dogs won't bark, and I know how to get him to his room noiselessly. At one time we had the same mistress. She was a lovely girl who asked so little. I was then working with the American army. The girl needed a winter coat. All I could give her was an old army blanket. She dyed it, cut a pattern from her old coat, and made herself a beautiful winter coat. And then she went off to Paris to spend a few days' leave with the Consul, in my army blanket. When her sister got married, I bought them a silk parachute (at that time they were made of silk, not nylon). The whole family sat down and out of the parachute they made a beautiful wedding dress, underwear, panties and petticoats for the whole family, and finally a nightgown for the bride. How I love to think of all those lovely girls wrapped up in parachute silk. I had a dream that they all floated through the sky, and came down to visit me in my lonely army cot."

When he had delivered Renate to her home, he gave her his card: "You can always call on Emile, the painter from Marseilles, if you have any secret missions, secret love missions to accomplish. I am discretion itself."

One day the Consul's wife asked Renate and Bruce to take her to the American desert which she had never seen. They agreed to drive her there. The Consul's wife packed a wicker basket with a picnic lunch. The wicker clasp was broken so she slipped a pencil through the noose. For the desert she wore sandals as worn as the Turkish rugs and loose fitting clothes which seemed like pale echoes of former Oriental wear.

Was it the American desert she had come to see or was she in her mind, superimposing over it the deserts of China, Africa, India, and this one a background upon which to weave reconstructions of past scenes, drum beats by an open fire, horse's hoofs and Arab shouts, while lambs roasted on a spit at night, black tents and midnight blue robes, black eyes and shining beards?

She was appreciative of the American desert but Renate did not know if she was using it like her worn rugs as a framework upon which to reweave more luxuriant scenes and wilder musical accompaniments.

Bruce was singing Western songs for her, accompanied by

his guitar. The pure voice of a young man who had never known the raucous tones of passion, the wild cries of battle, fever, pain, despair, lust. She lost herself in the songs which matched his flawless beauty. Was he evoking for her other songs, other guitars, other young men?

With those who had lived such full lives it was difficult to know which one they were evoking at the moment, and how much of past colors they were using to paint the present with. Did she see signboards, motels, coffee shops, giant hot dog signs, or mirages, ochre sand dunes, and vermilion sunsets?

"How strange it is," she said, "this beautiful desert seems uninhabited, as if the people living on it did not belong here. As if all of us were tourists!"

Then she talked about the Consul. The pattern of their marriage was frayed. The silver, gold, purple, red and green threads were worn away. What was left was her knowledge that he was possessed by his mother's spirit who had willed him first of all to be a war hero, then to surpass Don Juan with women. He had dutifully proceeded to fulfil all her wishes. He had brought her his war scar and his medals. But before he could present her with his prize for the best novel of the year, she had died.

The Consul's wife had played the role of substitute mother almost to perfection. She admired military prowess, she collaborated in his writing, she took pride even in his lover's prowess. She shared his love of politics, history, languages. She was at one with his ambitions. Her English coolness saved him from tears and clinging. She thought they would remain life companions if not bed companions.

Every scene between them was a witty charade. She always held the door open and he never left.

But it was only in Los Angeles that he began to talk about adopting a daughter. All these years while they travelled and he wrote his books, he had not thought about children. But now he felt he needed a daughter.

The Consul's wife had smiled and said: "That should be

89

simple nowadays. There are so many orphans in the world, in Korea, in Hungary, in Poland."

But the Consul protested: "Oh, no, oh, no. I don't want an undernourished, a deficient, pathetic, anaemic war victim in the house. I want a tanned, healthy, American child."

The Consul's wife was telling Renate and Bruce this story.

"He means Lolita," said Renate.

The Consul's wife remembered that in Turkey in moments of crisis, she had smoked opium. The poet Michaux had described how it was hashish which gave the illusion of levitation, and that it was from taking the drug that the legend of the "flying carpets" had originated. It was a flying carpet she needed now. But she knew of no opium den in Los Angeles, so friends gave her a tranquilizer.

She lay on her canopied bed and waited for its effects, waited to be wafted away from the Consulate.

"The opposite happened. I felt myself growing heavier and more passive. I felt myself turning into a white slug."

In spite of the tranquilizers, the Consul's wife realized that the adoption of an American daughter, a healthy American orphan, had subtly developed into an expedition into the realm of nubile youth from which he might never return, for it was he who had been adopted by a young film star. She began to wonder if their story were finished.

She remembered a day in Morocco, when she sat in a café and while waiting for the Consul to end a conference, had been embroidering a *petit point* tapestry. The Moroccans had gathered around her to watch her as they watched other craftsmen working the streets. She was using all the colored wools they loved, and her needlework was nimble. She worked on a small square and was but halfway done. One of the Moroccans in long black robes, with a dignified bearing, bent over her and whispered: "Would the lady give me this embroidery in memory of her fair hands at work? I have never seen such fair hands at work."

The Consul's wife had been startled by the request. She had

never parted with her embroideries. They covered all the chairs at the Consulate for many years. And all she could think to say was: "But it is not finished."

The Moroccan did not ponder this very much or very long. He almost immediately answered: "But dear lady, according to the Koran, nothing is ever finished."

Nothing is ever finished.

Yet there at her feet lay an open magazine with a photograph of the Consul and the young film star in a gondola in Venice. And the young film star had commented to the press that she did not believe in the European system of a wife and mistress in close collaboration.

Nothing is ever finished. As they had always shared and paralleled their interests, the study of dialects from all the provinces of India, the Tibetan *Book of the Dead*, the history of Turkey, the classification of Arabian war cries, the history of rugs and pottery of Egypt, the history of ship building, birds of Africa, diseases of Tahiti, would she now parallel his experience and fall in love with someone like Bruce, the masculine counterpart of the Consul's new love?

Could she love such an unstormy sky as his eyes, such a downy and untarnished skin, such a candid smile?

The man she carried in her mind at the moment was a Turkish war hero, a dark and wild man. She was writing his biography. The magnetic pull of his violence was greater than that of innocence and serenity.

A romance with a man who had died long ago promised at least no pain, no separations, no betrayals.

She boarded a plane to his native city.

Few people knew about him, but she knew him as well as if she had been his wife. She was adept at resuscitating a human being out of dusty books and files and letters in library vaults.

When she arrived at the Capitol, at the big hotel, she asked about ways to reach the village birthplace of Shumla. She was told she would have to wait for a guide, that no woman could

91

travel there alone, and that it was the middle of the day, time for a siesta and that she should rest and wait.

But she could not sleep, and she could not wait. The photograph of Shumla which she carried in her wallet was so vivid, so alive, that she felt as if she had an appointment with him which could not be postponed.

She slipped out of the hotel and walked to the bus stop, asking her way. The buses were taking their load of men, women, babies and animals. She was the last to climb on. She was the only pale, fair-haired woman aboard.

Nothing is ever finished. The Consul was walking into the future with his young film star, learning to dance jazz in caverns without windows, studying *The Dictionary of Slang*, helping to compose instant films; and the Consul's wife was retrogressing to the seventeenth century. Was this a form of faithfulness in her?

The bus jogged along. She was not treated like a tourist as her clothes were loose, crumpled and anonymous. She asked the conductor for Shumla's village. He was surprised she would want to stop there. A small village, half in ruins. No foreigners, no hotels, no guides. She persisted and he stopped the bus. The road was white with sun and dust, as white as a ski slope. The stones like chalk. No shade from the silvery, denuded, thirsty pepper and olive trees. A few women in black carrying baskets and pottery, or standing by the well. Streets of earth or rough stones. Her heel broke. She tore both heels off. She wrapped her neck scarf around her hair. She walked alone while half of the village slept through the heat of noon. Now and then she stopped to ask someone: "The house of Shumla?" Some would look blank and suspicious. Others pointed the way. It was outside the village. From inside the shops whose entrances were covered with strings of beads which sang in the breeze, people watched the pale-faced woman stumbling over stones. She finally arrived at a group of half-ruined houses. There was no sign. But someone said: "That's Shumla's house."

The big wooden door was open, because the hinges were half

rusted and half gone. The house had been built around a patio. The garden was taken care of; it had flowers and bushes and fruit trees in bloom. But the rooms were in ruin. There were vestiges of murals. A few broken colonnades. The ceilings were gone, and trailing plants fell from the beams. The heat like a hypnotist made everything stand still as if deep in sleep. No leaf stirred. No voices were heard. His presence, six feet of dark brown flesh, heavy black hair and strong voice must have filled the fragile place. It was no wonder that though born there, he had run away to fight wars. And only came home to die.

His religion forbade biographies, photographs, records of personal lives. So she had found little to reconstruct his life. Whoever thought about him, or tried to make a living portrait of him would be struck with misfortune. But the Consul's wife felt that having already suffered a loss, she could not be cursed any further. What else could happen to her? So she was fearless. She sat on one of the stone benches and tried to relive his life. Ill, dying, he must have listened to the sound of the trickling fountain. He did not die in the middle of battle. Did he regret this? Charging, screaming, with a curved sword held high above his head, he might have died then. Who had been there to hold the large, heavy head? As she said this she heard footsteps. A figure dressed in black appeared behind a column. It was a girl about fourteen. Her face was dark, her eyes of a highly polished black. But her mouth was tender, and a soft smile never quite left her lips.

"I came to see the house of Shumla because I am writing a book about him."

"But it is forbidden," said the girl.

"In your country, yes, but outside your country people think he was a great man, a hero, one of the bravest, and they would like to know about his life."

"People dared to write about him?"

"Not his own people, but scholars and historians. They are embalmers. They are taxidermists. I wanted to write about the

93

living man. I loved him. What do they know about him here in the village?"

"He was born here, in this house. I am a descendant of his. His great grandchild looks like him, they say. Come in and have tea with us."

At the back of the house in ruins, in a wing preserved from decay, she found a complete family, great grandparents, silent and like mummies, grandparents, grandchildren.

They served her tea. They read her manuscripts. They said: "You have been truthful. You have not done him harm. You really know him." It was the young girl who knew English and who translated it for them.

They invited her to stay a few days.

She slept in his bed. She saw his costumes, his swords, his knives, his shoulder bags, his bugle, his horse's saddles and silver ornaments. She saw his boots, his shawls, his tents, his carpets for sleeping, his blankets for the cold, his fur-rimmed hats, his necklaces, his medals, his spurs.

The great grandchild who was said to look like him, like Shumla at fifteen, loved horses and war, and could reproduce the special cries they had for battle. He sang the songs they sang around the campfires.

She saw the rough maps he had used, the rough notes, the messages, and many drawings of the period which portrayed battles, executions, punishments, ceremonials, victories, banquets, weddings, burials, decorations of heroes.

There were no clocks in the house, no calendars. It facilitated her return to the past, a long journey. It washed away the years from her body.

She lived with Shumla; he visited her in her dreams. Even though the times dictated ferocity towards the enemy and no mercy towards prisoners, his obedience to them had been tempered with as much mercy as he could display without being branded a woman.

She took many notes from their stories. She convinced the

family that Shumla, as a symbol of courage, belonged to the world, that it was not desecration to expose his life.

The old people had a wonderful memory. They remembered every detail they had heard, the color of his horse, the color of his belt, the number of beads on his necklace for luck, the names of his comrades, his friends, his relatives in other countries, the name of every battle, of every place where he had been.

When she left them, they made her promise to return. She carried a brief case filled with precious notes, letters, sketches. She had an intimate knowledge of the man. His stature, his fierceness, his valor made the modern world seem tame and fearful.

But the plane caught fire a few minutes before they landed. The pilot sent messages through the intercom. "If we can land before the second motor catches fire we will be safe. We only have four minutes to go. Please do not panic."

One minute. Two minutes. Three minutes. Four minutes.

They landed and stepped out through the emergency door. A fire engine and an abulance awaited them. The plane was emptied without accident, but the fire raged after they left it, and in this fire burned the intimate personal data on Shumla which his jealous religion, his jealous gods, did not wish to release to the press, to the world, to women like the Consul's wife who committed adultery in their dreams.

Colonel Tishnar came to Paradise Inn for dinner. If Renate had wanted to make a portrait of him it would have had to be a collage for he seemed made of all textures except human skin, human hair. His white hair could have been made of spun glass, his skin of sand-colored suede, his slim military figure of some new suave plastic.

His language too was stylized and every word glazed with patina. Long service with the British Intelligence Service had given him a stance which reminded one of photographs of T. E. Lawrence. He had known Lawrence, and shared with him a love of adventure, freedom, exile and poetry.

Colonel Tishnar had the gift of distilling from his own life only the humorous aspects. Having excluded illness, danger, tragedy, and personal relationships, his life appeared enchanted and pure fiction. His stories were perfect for dinner parties and they disturbed no one's digestion.

This evening he was a guest of a famous producer and they were planning to go on a safari together. The producer was asking him about the idiosyncrasies of lions.

"Well," said Colonel Tishnar, "I can tell you one story which will give you an idea of the fastidiousness of lions in general. Did you ever know Mrs. Larabee? I was with her on a safari. Mrs. Larabee had never resorted to the magic of dress or cosmetics, to any artificial effort to reconstruct herself. She may have decided at the beginning of her life that no charm or art could enhance her bold features, her straw-dry hair, her skin grained like sandpaper. We were lion hunting in Nairobi. As you probably know, the rule in this sort of hunting is to remain in the jeep and to keep on driving. Two natives accompanied Mrs. Larrabee, one to drive the jeep, the other to carry her gun. Somehow or other, her jeep became separated from the rest of the caravan. When it reached a shallow gully the engine stopped. While it was being repaired Mrs. Larrabee went for a walk along the bank. She was far out of sight and walking back meditatively when she noticed across the dry river bed an enormous lion walking parallel to her at the same pace. Mrs. Larrabee remained calm. She continued to walk towards her jeep. So did the lion. They both reached a bend in the gully. Towards the right was the road back to the jeep.

"Towards the left was the jungle. And here the lion calmly walked into the jungle and disappeared. But before the parting of the ways he looked at Mrs. Larrabee rather wistfully, as if to say goodbye. Mrs. Larrabee told me the story. She wanted me to explain what had saved her from being devoured. I could not explain it. The lion may have decided that Mrs. Larrabee's skin and boniness belonged to a new species of animal which did not tempt him. It may have been that he had already eaten and that there was nothing here to stimulate his appetite. Anyhow, what I could not tell Mrs. Larrabee was that if I had been the lion, and if I had met her walking along the edge of that gully, I too would have continued to walk in the opposite direction, wouldn't you?"

Once during the evening he paused in the middle of a story as if the end were no concern of his, and he had to be reminded to continue until he reached the climax.

"The end, you want an end," he said. "It may be I have lived too long with the Moroccans, and I have come to believe as they believe that nothing ends, nothing is ever finished."

"What about the adventurer's life? Does he always remain alone? Will you every marry?"

"I could only marry if I could find a woman who has had as rich a life as mine. Then I would be willing to stay at home, and sit by the fireside, and we would both tell each other of our endless adventures and relive them all."

"I know exactly the woman for you," said Renate. "She has had as adventurous a life as yours. T. E. Lawrence carried her books of poems with him, she visited him in the desert, and I am sure you were at the same places, knew the same people, made the same voyages."

"But never at the same time," said Colonel Tishnar. "This lack of synchronization augurs badly for a marriage. Already I ask myself was she always late? I never could bear to wait for a woman."

"She has just arrived," said Renate.

Tessa's dress was airy, of a black transparent material stiffened by chemistry as organdie had once been by starch and ironing. It gave her the crisp silhouette of a young woman. The enormous bow on her breast seemed like wings which would carry her off at any moment. Her hair, though grey, was glossy and electric, and the ends curled in the air like feathers at full mast. Her dress, the stance of her high-heeled shoes, reflected the alertness of her spirit. Her laughter and her voice were young and supple. Age could wrinkle her skin, freckle her hands, ruthlessly weigh down her eyelids, but it could not deaden her fervor, her mobility, her obedience to every challenge of life.

As soon as she was introduced to Colonel Tishnar she began a story: "I have just come back from my gold mine in Ghost Town. I bought it when they discovered a cheaper way of treating the low grade ore discarded by the old miners. All I have to do is climb a ladder down the shaft, from my very own cellar, pick up enough ore, treat it in this new acid, just enough of it to spend in the evening at the famous gambling table of the old pioneers. Ghost Town is coming back to life. The old saloon is still decorated with red damask walls and a crystal chandelier brought from France when wealth first came to the miners. One can live and gamble on ten dollars a day. I am going to invite all my artist friends to come and live with me there. The only difficulty with this plan is that I have lost their confidence. During the war I offered some of the homesick surrealists a way to sail back to Europe. I bought a ship for them at auction. It was in New Orleans. And I invited all those who wanted to sail to come with me. But the ship sank in the harbor; before they even boarded it. Some of them may have thought it was a plot against surrealism."

When Tessa left, Colonel Tishnar whispered to Renate: "What

a pathetic woman. All flutter and furbelows, no meaning to her life, all chaos."

Renate spent a sleepless night. For she knew that Tessa, too, had been searching for the man who had enough stories to tell to make their staying at home not seem like a retirement from active life. And she was ill with a bad heart. How could Renate inform her that Colonel Tishnar had decided to leave that very day for India? Could her old heart bear this defeat, she who was not familiar with failure? She would expect Colonel Tishnar to call her up. Her charm had never failed. But it was Renate who called in her warmest, most exultant voice: "Colonel Tishnar thought you absolutely charming, too charming in fact. He told me you reminded him of his dead wife, who made him suffer a great deal and who was unfaithful to him. He is leaving for India. He told me you are far too dangerous for his peace of mind."

Tessa's voice grew lighter and younger, even though the tired heart caused breathlessness between each sentence. She was elated to think that Colonel Tishnar had run away so far from her power and charm.

"And do you know, Renate, I think he is right. I am sure I would have been unfaithful to him."

So there was Colonel Tishnar already won, married, and betrayed, all in a few hours, a victory to stimulate the failing heart of any woman.

Renate grew tired of painting portraits, of hostessing, of designing dresses, and so she made a plan for a new magazine.

She designed a dummy copy to show unbelievers. The theme of the cover and of the contents of the magazine was freedom, freedom of imagination, of expression, of style, of subject. Each time she talked with a friend she found a secret cache of sparkling ideas which he or she had been unable to utilize. There was Max the photographer. During the day he visited furniture shops and put together kitchens for television advertisements. He employed models who demonstrated cake mixes. He had to construct a new set every day, photograph it, and begin anew the next day with a model shampooing her hair, or a child playing with a new toy on an indestructible carpet. But at night he went out with his camera and shot a secret Los Angeles very few people knew. He had a portfolio filled with startling pictures turned down by other magazines as *way out* because they were out of the way of people who never left their offices.

John was a clairvoyant film critic and he wrote for Renate describing all the beautiful and original scenarios written by writers of quality which lay in "cold storage" in the studios. He also wrote a dazzling article made up of all the paragraphs which had been lopped off at the beginning, in the middle or sometimes at the end for the sake of layout.

Judith Sands offered several stories which were too long or too short for other magazines, and which did not tie up with any journalistic news item like a play on Broadway, a film in Hollywood, or a murder, or burglary or a leap from the fifteenth floor.

Several novelists had beautiful chapters left out of their novels. The novels had been weighed on a scale and found to be two ounces overweight.

Betty was dressing dummies for Saks windows, but she was skilled in lively and seductive layouts. She did not split stories into fifteen to-be-continued columns interrupted with gaudy advertisements. She quarantined commercials.

Henri offered his most secret recipes.

Harry sold records in a music store, and had stored in his mind the most complete knowledge of jazz music and its composers.

Renate was inviting contributions born of enthusiasm, inventiveness, novelty, exploration, of people in love with their media and whose love was contagious. What she banished was the bored critics, the imitators, the second-handers, the standardized clichés. Even the first dummy aroused in people a feeling they were at last to know, read, see everything other magazines neutralized, dissolved, synthesized, deodorized, sterilized, disguised, monotonized, mothproofed, and sprayed with life-repellents.

"It must be alive," was Renate's only editorial principle.

Alive like Don Bachardy's line portraits of personalities, like Renate's women and animals, like Judith Sands' stories of cities and the lovers who had lived in them, or the Consul's wife's selection of how writers had written about women dressing (or undressing) and a thousand other scintillating subjects which other editors believed radioactive.

Renate advertised for capital. The very same evening she received a telephone call: "My name is John Wilkes. I am answering your advertisement. I like the idea of your magazine. I am 27 years old. I made my money in oil wells in Phoenix. Send me the dummy. Here is my address. But do not telephone me. It makes me nervous. I am always on the go for business. I never know where I am going to be. Send me a budget for what you will need to run for a year. Tomorrow I fly to New York for a conference. The next day I may be in Egypt. I am bored with business and welcome a new interest."

Renate posted the dummy. The young millionaire telephoned again: "I am in New York. I received the dummy. I like your ideas. Keep working on them. As soon as I can I will fly to Los Angeles and meet your staff and your lawyer. Tell your lawyer to prepare a rough draft of the contract."

Renate made the usual inquiry about Mr. John Wilkes. The

answer was: "Unknown." But it was suggested that John Wilkes might have accounts in the name of his company. Or perhaps not in Phoenix at all. So Renate relinquished the search for credit references.

Manuscripts began to arrive, cartoons, letters, recordings to review, books to review, passes to film openings, theatre openings. Renate and her staff were invited to fashion shows, exhibitions, to travel at half-rates to Paris, to visit film stars, to interview visitors from Japan.

They all gave up their routine jobs. Renate had cards printed with their various titles. Every morning enough original material arrived to fill a magazine each day.

John Wilkes was still busy, flying here and there, but always telephoning, always interested. He sent a photograph of himself. He looked as Gary Cooper looked at his age.

Renate rented an office. Friends helped her to decorate it. The symbol of it was a mobile. Several mobiles hung from the ceiling, setting the theme of liveliness and motion of the magazine.

In a few weeks they were in touch with all the countries they had wanted to visit, all the personalities they had wanted to know. It was if everyone responded to the ebullience and felt attracted to the atmosphere not yet desiccated by story conferences and dehydrated by editorial policies. Secret wishes and fantasies were being materialized. Every encouraged idea generated a new one. Renate could hardly contain the richness. It was like an oil well which had overflowed. Circulation problems? Only a problem of circulation of the blood.

John Wilkes applauded, laughed, shared in the universe born of *yes*. He sponsored Renate's gaiety and originality, her belief that ideas must only be handled by the one who gave birth to them or else they withered.

"Is it time for a celebration?" they asked.

Renate said: "Let's wait until John Wilkes comes. Let's wait until the contracts are signed."

But they bought champagne. It was such a delight to buy

champagne and fill in a slip which would be paid by the expense account. No more concern over narrow personal budgets. What a delight to take a taxi when carrying heavy portfolios and charge it. What a delight to eat in a new restaurant every day and be treated like a millionaire so one would write flatteringly about the dinner. What delight to visit the printer all of them knew, and to be able to say to him they would pay him handsomely this time. What delight to plan for Christmas in June, to reserve hotel rooms for the film festivals at Venice, to plan for Spoleto, to accept invitations to the jazz festivals.

John Wilkes arrived. He and Renate spent three whole days with lawyers. Renate looked tired but elated. "He says yes to *everything*."

In the climate of enthusiasm, new ideas proliferated.

At last the contracts were done with. The young millionaire had consented to everything. He had also agreed to meet the staff, and to have champagne with them. They were to gather at Renate's house.

The sun gold-leafed the sea, the tips of the leaves, the window panes, the pottery and the paintings. Cars arrived. Everyone seemed to feel lighter, to walk more confidently.

Bruce brought Renate an umbrella for her trip to Paris. It was made of cellophane, and planted with bunches of plastic violets. To walk in the rain and yet be able to see the sky, the buildings, the people. And her face behind it when she opened it was like the face of a mermaid in an aquarium. The violets seemed planted in her dark hair.

But John Wilkes did not arrive. The telephone rang. He excused himself. He had been called to a conference in Denver. Anyway, he had to take the contracts to his own committee and mail the checks to close the deal.

There was a moment of suspense.

"Oh, we mustn't be superstitious," said Renate, "that's how millionaires behave. They are always in business conferences. They have no time for celebrations."

They drank the champagne, but for the first time their gathering seemed more like the gathering of other magazine staffs, sol-emn and cautious.

The next day there was silence and suspense, as if the post office, the telegraph office, the bank, and the postman must not be disturbed in the performance of their duties. They did not telephone each other with new ideas.

On each desk there was a pile of unpaid bills. On Renate's desk a bill from the printer for the dummy, writing paper and cards, and a bill for the rental of the office.

Each one had a personal, intimate problem he did not want to share with the others: doctor's bills, insurance bills, a parent to support, all the obligations which were going to be met with money earned while doing what they loved to do. An unknown writer had seen his name on the cover. An unknown singer had believed herself discovered.

But no check came.

Renate broke her promise not to telephone John Wilkes. But when she did he took a long time to come to the telephone. His answers for the first time, sounded vague and evasive.

Renate asked her lawyer's advice. The lawyer spoke to his neighbor who worked for the F.B.I. Quiet investigations were made. Two weeks had passed since John Wilkes had signed the contracts and promised a check.

It was then Renate discovered that the young millionaire was a gardener in a millionaire's home in Phoenix. He liked to play the role of millionaire. He had done it before. He had been in New York, had been present at several conferences over new projects, studied them, signed contracts, and vanished.

Renate could imagine him clipping rose bushes and listening to the talk of rich oil men resting on chaises-longues around their pools: "I am investing in Playboy. I am producing a play. I am backing a film."

And Renate could see the young, shy, handsome gardener, studying the roles he was to play while watering the lawns and planting bushes. He had learned a trade which gave him elation and a sense of power. He had done it well.

104

When she telephoned him the telephone was probably right in the kitchen, or in the tool house where people could hear him. And the genuine millionaires were probably sitting a few yards away, planning other investments.

There was no law to jail a man who swindled one of illusions and not of money. The gardener watered other people's dreams. It was not his fault that they grew so big and had to be pruned.

RENATE AND LISA HAD MET IN ACAPULCO WHEN SHE WAS THERE for a few days designing a mural for the new hotel.

She was sitting in the dining-room when she saw a Toulouse-Lautrec figure walk down the stairs, a Toulouse-Lautrec with a Rousseau jungle for a background. Renate's eyes were also caught by the brilliant native color of her dress. She used Mexican textiles. She wore jewelry copied from the Aztec days of gold exuberance. The bouffant hair was not in fashion then, but she wore it naturally, and it made her face small and delicate. She had a small straight nose such as one only sees in paintings, eyes always mocking, a slender neck and a fine head attached surprisingly to a voluptuous body. Her body was heavy but in the way of primitive women, that is, not inert but alive and rhythmic, graceful and vibrating. Her movements had a vivacity and a flow and something more; she had provocative movements, as if she were about to undress. She rolled her hips, her shoulders, like a strip-teaser about to slide out of her clothes. She had the swinging roll of sailors and prostitutes suggesting the rocking of ships or of beds. She thrust her breasts out as if she would separate herself from them and fly off. Her hands would rest on different parts of her body as if to indicate where the eyes should alight. She shook her head, alert and animal, and laughed with a ripple which ran through her whole body. It was as if she kept dancing just enough to keep her jewelry tinkling and her earrings swinging.

Renate and Lisa talked on the terrace at night after dinner while waiting to see what the evening would bring. In spite of her two children, a girl of seven and a boy of nine, the men treated her as if she were a young woman. Her laughter was inviting as she lay on the chaise-longue, eclipsing the vivid tropical flowers, petal soft, perfumed among the dark heavy tropical foliage. But her exotic plumage did not seem a permanent part of her. One felt she was uncomfortable within it, and that her natural state was nudity.

She could flirt and tease and laugh with people she did not like, like a professional. She never conserved or economized her charms, or refused anyone the fullness of her laughter, or the long glance into her igniting eyes, or proximity to her tanned skin. Acapulco was a perfect background for her. Her skin was naturally swarthy and she seemed like a native, in harmony with the climate, never too warm, never estranged from it, never intimidated by darkness, strange bird voices, monkey chatter, or the sudden discovery of an iguana practising camouflage and almost invisible, frozen in the sun, the color of the rock it lay on.

When Diego Rivera painted her, with his Mexican brush, he made her mouth twice as thick, her nose twice as wide, her eyes twice as large, adding fierceness, and it was no longer Lisa, because Lisa was this paradox between a jungle-luxuriant body and a delicate Toulouse-Lautrec head.

In Acapulco no one ever thought of profession, titles, background, or past history. Everyone lived in the present and looked at each other with an appreciation of appearance only as one looked at the sea, the mountains, lagoons, birds, animals, flowers. Races, classes, fortunes, all blended into an object for the pursuit of pleasure. Swimming, sunning, dancing, idleness, made people part of the scenery, for the pleasure of the eyes only. Quality was a matter of contribution to the beauty of the spectacle. This unique qualification was determined by how one looked walking down the stairs to the dining-room, because spotlights had been planted between the cactus and the palms, and the descent, and pause, just before entering the dining room was like a small stage, high above the diners, well lighted, and well designed so that hundreds of eyes could determine if this figure was, or was not, an aesthetic contribution to the isle of pleasure. Anyone at this moment could achieve membership into the club of the *deshabillés*.

Lisa's origins were even more obscured by her knowledge of many languages, of many countries, her exotic costumes, her home in Acapulco, her rootlessness, her several husbands no one had known, her mysterious income.

Anyone seeking to include her in a realistic novel would have had to resort, even against the grain, to impressionism. Her Mexican servants treated her as one of their own because she ate their food. A Mexican god was cemented on a column in her garden. There were no books in her house, but many canvasses and supplies of paints.

Having situated her in Mexico permanently in her memory, Renate was all the more startled to run into her on Third Avenue, New York, before the elevated was removed. Lisa was carrying a brown shopping bag. Her hair so wild and abundant was hidden by a handkerchief. For a moment, in the striped light of soot-filtered sun, Renate wondered if all she remembered had belonged to Acapulco and not to Lisa, for she could not find in Lisa herself any gleams of gold, of sun, no tinkling of bracelets, no pearly laughter. Lisa wore a dark winter coat and seemed to have amalgamated with the city and the winter.

"Renate! What are you doing in New York?"

"I'm having an exhibition on 57th Street. And you, Lisa?"

"Do you remember the Acapulco sailing and fishing contests? Well, Bill was with one of the newspapers, a reporter for *Field and Stream*. He came in his trailer to cover the celebration. I had just finished building my house and I had a housewarming. We began to dance together Sunday night, the night of the prize distribution, and we continued to dance together for two or three nights. I don't remember that we stopped for meals. I had just divorced my third husband, and I felt like beginning a completely new cycle. But I couldn't persuade Bill to stay. Instead he gave me an hour to get ready and took me away in his trailer. We went from Acapulco to Fraser, Colorado, on another assignment. I arrived there with gold sandals, and it was snowing. While Bill covered his story, I waited for him in a cafeteria and played the slot machines. All my life I had dreamed of finally settling in Acapulco and living there and going native. And here I was in a snowstorm, sleeping and traveling in a trailer on my way to New York."

As they talked, Lisa led Renate to a small and shabby apartment house. They walked to the top floor.

"Bill is poor because most of his salary goes in alimony."

When the elevated passed they had to stop talking. This gave Renate time to wonder why Lisa had not clung to her beautiful life.

When they reached the top floor, instead of a dark, anonymous door, Renate found a canary yellow garden gate. Lisa had covered the walls of the hallway with lattice of vine-covered trellis; the ceilings hung with potted plants and cages filled with singing birds. When she touched the gate Mexican bells chimed. Lisa shed her dark coat and appeared in a flaming orange dress. The small apartment was no longer in New York. Rugs, panels, murals, paintings, statues, sarapes, white fur on the bed. It was Acapulco. She had placed her stone gods in niches, her jewelry overflowed from a coffer, and a record player spun tender Mexican songs.

There were Mexican paper flowers in a jar, silks on the windows, and the shutters were painted yellow so that even on this dark day the sun seemed to be shining. There were more birds singing in the small kitchen.

This gallant effort at transplantation touched Renate. Would Lisa survive in this illusory set? Bill had torn her away but had not won her to his own life. What quality did he possess that she should be willing to risk withering her essentially primitive and tropical nature?

"Bill has gone for liquor," said Lisa. "He will bring back my sister who lives nearby."

At this moment they both arrived. Bill was small, not handsome, and he was cursing the chiming bells over the door and the wicker gate which clung to his coat. His tie was askew, his coat rumpled, and the end of an unlit cigar hung from his lips. He was in harmony with Third Avenue, and so was his harsh accent, and his way of exaggerating his homeliness and bad manners as if he were proud of them. Lisa's sister had the accent of a street boy, and the impersonal mechanized politeness of a telephone operator. Both of them talked to Lisa as if she were a pretender, as if everything she wore, or said, or hung on the walls were artificial, not hers by birth.

Bill put his short, stocky hand on Lisa's knee and said smiling at Renate: "Well, isn't it good to be home again? One of these days you'll throw out all this fancy foreign stuff and be yourself again."

"Home?" asked Renate.

"Home, yes," said Bill. "Lisa lived around the corner from here when we were kids. We played in this street together. I was the first boy who kissed her. We had not seen each other for twenty years. She wanted me to stay in Acapulco and live her life, with all those phonies talking languages I couldn't understand. I didn't think she'd bring all this stuff with her. I can't bring my friends here for a game of cards."

Lisa's sister said: "We both worked in the same office. The trouble started when she won a painting scholarship to Mexico. It all went to her head. She married an oil man. And then a man with a yacht big enough to sail to Europe."

And because the paintings, the plants, the statues, the flowers and birds had been transplanted, not born there, they began to seem as they talked, like a background for a painting, and Lisa herself a model hired for one afternoon to sit for a painter, and Bill and Lisa's sister like boors who had entered a gallery by mistake, expecting pictures of horses and trout fishing and found themselves in a dream painted by Rousseau, a couch in the middle of the jungle.

Would Bill and his card-playing friends be able to cage Lisa? Her cage now would be the stripes of dusty sunlight falling through the rails of the Third Avenue Elevated trains.

Bill shut off the record player before the Mexican song was finished.

Bill had come and awakened her from her dream of Acapulco ·

110

with a cigar flavored kiss from the ashcan painting period of her childhood.

THE BELL RANG. IT WAS DOCTOR MANN WITH FLOWERS FOR LISA and a cigar for Bill.

He was collecting paintings to exhibit in Israel. He wanted to borrow some of Lisa's Mexican paintings.

He had heard about Renate's paintings and said he would be proud to take some back with him.

But he was not a painting fetichist. His particular hobby was quite exceptional.

Once a year Doctor Mann flew from Israel on a mysterious mission. But his leisure time he spent in visiting women writers. One by one he visited them all. He brought them brandy and chocolates from Israel, books to sign for his collection of auto-graphed editions, and kissed them only once on parting.

He boasted of these friendships as other men boast of sexual conquests.

Many of these visits required patience, diplomacy and re-search work. First of all, to find their addresses, and then some-one who might introduce him, and then to obtain an appoint-ment, and, most difficult of all, to gain the privilege of a tête à tête.

His hair grew grey. His library of dedicated books was rich in treasures.

Just as Don Juan was always eager to test his charm on frigid women, Doctor Mann finally encountered the most inaccessible of all women writers and felt challenged to woo her.

He heard that Judith Sands was not only difficult to meet but that she avoided everyone related to the literary world. She led a secluded life in the Village, New York, and it was rumored that she preferred obscure village bars and anonymous company.

A few bar addicts vaguely remembered talking with a woman called Judith Sands but they insisted that she talked like a truck driver and could not possibly have written the poetic and stylized mythological novel she was praised for.

Those who lived in Paris before the war remembered a handsome, red-haired amazon in a tailored suit who sat at the Dôme.

A few who lived in the Village knew her, but no one had anything to say, no revelations, no messages, as if those who knew her practised a sick room secrecy, as if she had sealed their lips. There was an unnatural silence around her, either because she had satirized everyone, which she was known to do, or because those who respected her work did not wish to expose a Judith who did not resemble her parabolic work.

Several of the flat-soled women in tailored suits who walked down Eighth Street could have been Judith Sands. In an age of glaring, crude limelight, she had been able to avoid all familiarity, and her anonymity was preserved by an invisible repellent.

It was as if her novel had been the story of an earthquake by one of its victims; the book once written, and the author with it, seemed to have fallen into a crevice.

This shadowy figure aroused Doctor Mann's love of conquest.

He bought a bottle of champagne and rushed to the address he had been given. There was no name on the bell to the apartment, but he had been told that she lived on the second floor. Doctor Mann climbed the dark stairway and knocked on a dark door. No answer.

He waited and knocked again.

Silence.

He paced the frayed rug. He stared with an ironic smile at the empty niche where the stairway made a turn. When the Village was Italian, the statue of a saint had nestled there. He sat down inside the niche and waited. His ear caught a rustle inside, and it was enough to encourage his verbal gallantry.

He began an interminable monologue like one of the characters in her novel.

Every novelist knows that at one time or another he will be confronted with the incarnation of one of his characters. Whether that character is based on a living person or not, it will draw into its circle those who resemble it. Sooner or later the portrait will attract its twin, by the magnetism of narcissism, and the author will feel this inhabitant of his novel come to life and hear his character speaking as he had imagined.

And so, Doctor Mann, in the same fast liquid monologue she had set down, picked up his own story in Siberia where he had been sent for rebellion against the régime, and where there was nothing to nourish him except books; where his faith in woman's intuitive knowledge had made him translate Judith Sand's book into Hebrew; from there to his American wife and children in a modern apartment in Israel and his work with a newspaper which put him in touch with all the plays and books being written. "You know, my dear Judith Sands, I am not here to frighten you, or violate your privacy. I am not a man visiting a woman. I am a man with a profound love of words. In the words of the Talmud: 'Kaka' tuv . . . It is written.' I know you do not like strangers; but, just as you are no stranger to me, I cannot be a stranger to you because I feel that, in a sense, you gave birth to me. I feel you once described a man who was *me* before I knew who I was, and it was because I recognizd him that I was able to be myself. You will recognize me when you see me. I am sure you have already recognized how I think; this mixture in me which makes me feel my way through experience as women do, and yet talk even when I do not wish to talk like an intellectual, a scholar (which is mockery as I do not believe that they know as much as the poet in his delirium). I have grown grey hairs waiting to meet you. I could not find your address or anyone who knew you. Then a taxi driver told me he had just driven uptown a woman who talked as I did, with a man with an English accent, and he said they were going to the opening of his cocktail party; and then I knew you were in New York and had been with T. S. Eliot. Every word you wrote I ate, as if it was manna. Finding one's self in a book is a second birth; and you are the only one who knows that at times men behave like women and women like men, and that all these distinctions are mock distinctions, and that is why your doctor put on a wig when he wanted to talk about his loves, and I don't know why Thomas Mann wrote about

114

Transposed Heads for there are other transpositions of far greater interest, and your story is the most accurate in the world."

No answer.

But there was a creak of a chair, and a soft footstep on the floor behind the door.

Doctor Mann added: "I am leaving my gifts to you on the door mat. I hope you like champagne."

"I don't drink," said a low, deep voice behind the closed door.

"Well, you can offer it to your friends. Tomorrow I fly back to Israel at nine in the evening. I will come again at five o'clock. Perhaps you will open your door to a man who is going away. And you will see I am no stranger. Remember this, it is good for a writer to meet with the incarnation of a character he has invented. It gives him an affirmation, a substantial proof of his intuitions, divinations. Here I stand before you, talking as you said I might, and reminding you that what may have seemed a ghost in a dream, in your smoke-filled heart at night, is a man who got his knowledge and his degrees from books in a cell in Siberia, and who translated you by the light of a candle."

"Come back tomorrow. We'll have coffee together," said the voice.

The next day he came. But there was no answer to his knock and so he began his monologue: "When you deny me the presence of a writer, you really deny me a part of myself that has not yet been born, and whose existence I need to believe in. I always wanted to be a writer, but I talk too much, it evaporates, or it may be I have not yet decided whether to write as a man or as a woman. But you have been my writer self writing for me. I could talk wastefully, negligently, only because you were there preserving and containing my spirit. When you deny me your presence, you commit spiritual murder, for if I have been for years talking with your words, spending them lavishly, extravagantly, it was only because I believed I could always renew myself at the source. You may feel this was an imposition. No one should be forced to carry the unfulfilled self of another. But if you are so skilled with words and have already written *me*, in a sense you have stolen *me,* and must return what you stole. You must come out and say: 'I will go on writing for you, I will be your articulateness. I gave birth to you and I must grant you the fullest expansion of speech.' And you need me, Judith Sands. You must not stifle yourself behind closed doors. Solitude may rust your words. Silence is not your element. It will asphyxiate you. We need each other! We are indispensable to each other. I to your work and you to my life. Without me spending your words you may not be incited to mint new ones. I am the spendthrift and you the coiner. We cannot live completely apart. And if I speak your character on perhaps a lower key than you had intended, even perhaps with a few false notes, it is because I have never met a writer with perfect pitch. If you refuse to talk to a plain man like me, your ambiguities will become intolerably tenuous, like the end of your book, which I do not understand."

The door opened halfway. Judith Sands appeared shadowed against the light. Behind her, a chaotic lair, undistinguishable objects in wild disorder. She closed the door upon her cavernous dwelling and gave Doctor Mann her strong, firm hand.

"I am not absolutely certain of the meaning of that end to my book, but I am sure of one thing, that human beings can reach such desperate solitude that they may cross a boundary beyond which words cannot serve, and at such moments there is nothing left for them but to *bark.*"

As they walked together Doctor Mann asked: "Is it true what they say that you have written another book, that you keep it hidden in cartons under your bed, that no one has read it?"

"Yes, it is true."

"Why won't you let it be read, published? It will shatter your solitude."

"No, it will only aggravate it. The more they read of me, the louder they deny my existence, the existence of my characters. They say I have only described unique specimens."

"But I can show you how these specimens reproduced themselves. They are scattered over the world. I will take you to the places where I know your book is a perpetual house guest, always sitting in the library, a guest of honor. You will only meet those who nourished themselves on it, the descendants of your characters."

Doctor Mann observed how carefully Judith Sands had sought to efface in herself all traces of having been the woman once so wildly loved in her own novel. She had created a neutral appearance, wearing colors one would not notice nor remember, anonymous clothes, a cape which concealed the lines of her body, a Tyrolian hat with a feather on it. The feather, however, had retained its impertinence, from the days when she won every tournament with her wit.

"Solitude," said Doctor Mann, "is like Spanish moss which finally suffocates the tree it hangs on."

"Don't you think I have thought of that whenever someone slips a piece of paper under my door saying 'I love you Judith Sands'; don't you think I ask myself is this another come to love me and also destroy me? Another one staying out all night and with each step away from me wearing out the soles of my heart with waiting? Or another come to steal my own image of me and expose it to the world, distorted of course? Or another come to resuscitate parts of me which I have already buried?"

"But you and those you loved have children scattered all over the world. They are descendants in direct line from your creations. Aren't you curious about them?"

"How does one find them?"

"You can fly now and pay later. Jet by Alitalia, Bonanza, Lan Chile, the Comet Service, the Flying Tiger, Slick Airways, El Israel, Futura. You have your choice of names. Oh, I forgot the Pink Cloud Flights. We will visit only those who kept your book on the top shelf hidden from their parents, those who read it in other languages, in Dutch, Italian, German, Japanese, Yugoslavian, Hungarian, Russian, Flemish; those who read it and pretended they never heard of it but proceeded to live their lives oriented by its flow; those who succumbed to its contagion and searched for a similar atmosphere as if it were the only air they could breathe in; those who fell in love with your characters

117

and searched for their counterparts. Those who quoted it to each other as a password to enter a unique and exclusive world. We will only go where your book is a part of the furniture."

"What is going on tonight that we don't have to get on a jet to see?"

"I will take you to see Tinguely's Machine that Destroys Itself."

"I thought only dreamers destroyed themselves."

As they hailed a taxi she raised her head and watched a plane flying above them leaving a trail of smoke which took the shape of words: SEE THE GREATEST STORY EVER TOLD.

The courtyard of the Museum of Modern Art in New York; a winter night; the snow had already fallen; a blue mist came up from the pavement as if it were breathing.

In the courtyard of the museum stood a floodlighted pile of objects one could not at first identify, a pile of objects such as one might find in a junkyard: an old piano, a broken bicycle, a child's carriage with only three wheels, a broken ladder with only half its rungs, punctured tires, soap boxes, old bottles, odd pieces of machinery like those of an automobile cemetery.

The entire pile was painted chalk white; it looked like a mound of debris covered by snow. Hung on the scaffolding were large bottles of colored chemicals. A giant roll of paper hung ready to unroll, like a newspaper going through a printing press. A giant brush hung poised over it to write on it as on a ticker tape.

The entire structure was wired and several men were still testing the connections which would set it in motion. A huge balloon topped the edifice, and a torn umbrella opened over a fire extinguisher.

The public began to wander in, to stumble over the TV wires, to be blinded by flash bulbs.

In the icicle blue night the floodlights looked orange. Smoke came from everyone's mouths as they talked.

There was a tussle between a museum guard and a camera man who had climbed on one of the valuable statues and rested his camera bag on a valuable naked arm. Faces were violently lighted, cameras whirred, the wired structure seemed about to totter, the snow melted.

The fire chief in his uniform looked solemn and concerned. Tinguely himself was smiling and calm. When he had dragged his machines through the streets of Paris for an exhibition, had he not been arrested as the suspected designer of a new kind of destructive, death dealing instrument?

There was a rumble as of an advancing earthquake. Clattering, steaming, hiccoughing, vibrating, puffing, hissing, juggling, dislocating, trembling, the entire structure went into a spasm which opened the bottles of chemicals, and they exploded into colored smoke which filled the balloon with air, set the roll of paper unrolling and the brush painting erratically the names of the artists like stock market quotations. But before the list was finished, the roll of paper rolled backwards, perversely, and swallowed the names in desperate inversion.

The child's carriage detached itself from the mass of shaking, sputtering, burning structure, as if it wished to escape destruction. It rolled towards one of the spectators as if looking for a child in the audience. It carried a drum which played automatically. And then it returned, as if hypnotized by electronic umbilical cords, resigned to its fate, unable to escape. It made one more sortie towards the spectator, one more appeal from its drum, an appeal for life, and inevitably rolled back into the pyre.

The piano started to burn slowly, and as it burned the notes played wistfully, out of tune, unreal, like a pianola. The flames consumed the wood but not the notes and not the wires. The notes played like the cry of trapped music, hollow, expiring.

The whole structure rattled erratically, in counter-rhythms, steaming senselessly, all motions in reverse, each interfering with another, negating it, inverted activity, bending and twisting and tearing at itself, introverted activity ending sometimes in a deadlock so that the fire was allowed to spread more quickly. The ladder trembled, lost a few rungs, fell. The balloon at the very tip of the structure, a huge orange balloon, gasped and burst. The chemicals smoked green, orange and blue.

The paper with the names of artists unrolled again, a few more names were added, and then it swallowed them all again, finally catching fire.

It seemed at times like an infernal factory in which every operation had gone mad, in which the levers and buttons did the opposite of what they were designed to do, all the mechanisms reversed.

The fire devoured one more note of the piano, and only three notes were left playing. Then two. Then one which would not die.

The fire chief stood by, preoccupied, wondering at which moment the suicide of the machine would become an attempt to overthrow the government.

Smoke and winter's breath met in mid-air. The snow melted at the edges, but the white paint did not.

The piano played the last will and testament of a dying piano. The public pressed closer to hear its last melody. The fire chief picked up the fire extinguisher.

At this point the artist protested against the interrupted climax. The public hissed the fire chief. The artist said everything was under control, but the fire chief did not believe him. He began to extinguish the fire.

One more explosion of an orange chemical, one more balloon bursting, one more umbrella closing mournfully, one more piece of wood falling to the ground, one more tire rolling out of the pulsing machine, epilepsy of tin, turmoil, one more gasp, one more twist of metal, one more hiccough.

The fire chief interfered with the drama. He retarded the process. If the ladder had not burned he would have climbed on it to rescue the piano, the baby carriage. Suicide is illegal.

The skeleton of the mischievous dinosaur of the dump heap did not collapse; its suicide was about to fail. The artist gave a quick, discreet kick to the last supporting beam and then it collapsed, and the public moved closer to the smoking remains, picking up fragments for souvenirs, dismantling.

What the photographers caught was the kick.

THE CROWD DISPERSED. THE NEWSPAPERMEN WENT OFF TO WRITE their copy. Each person carried a piece of the white debris. Doctor Mann had rescued the roll of paper with the signatures of artists which had not burned. The name of Judith Sands was among them. As they stood in the corner hailing a taxi Renate and Bruce came out of the revolving door. Renate recognized Doctor Mann. When Doctor Mann introduced Judith Sands, Renate flung her arms around her.

"I love your book so much I have worn it down with readings; it looks like a pack of cards worn out by a gypsy fortune teller."

"We wanted to rescue the piano," said Renate. "I felt it still had a song in it. I didn't want to rescue anything dead."

"Let's sit somewhere and have a drink, and read the roll of artists' names."

Judith Sands said in a slightly rough voice: "Come back to my place. I have something to show you."

They followed her. In the dimly lit apartment they could only see paintings on the walls and many books. The only light came from a desk lamp. Judith Sands without taking her cape off, went to the couch, nudged two cats off who had been sleeping on it, got on her knees, pulled out a carton overflowing with papers, pulled out a bunch which had been clipped together and gave it to Renate to read.

It began:

"Vienna was the city of statues. They were as numerous as the people who walked the streets. They stood on the tip of the highest towers, lay down on stone tombs, sat on horseback, kneeled, prayed, fought animals and wars, danced, drank wine and read books made of stone . . ."